A Harvest of Ripe Figs

by Shira Glassman

A Harvest of Ripe Figs by Shira Glassman, edited by Jaymi Lynn

Esther of the Singing Hands is Perach's Sweetheart, a young and beautiful musician with a Girl Next Door image. When her violin is stolen after a concert in the capital city, she doesn't expect the queen herself to show up, intent upon solving the mystery.

But Queen Shulamit -- lesbian, intellectual, and mother of the six-month-old crown princess -- loves to play detective. With the help of her legendary bodyguard Rivka and her dragon, and with the support of her partner Aviva the Chef, Shulamit turns her mind toward the solution -- which she quickly begins to suspect involves the use of illegal magic that could threaten the safety of her citizens.

Tales from Outer Lands by Shira Glassman, edited by Jaymi Lynn
"Rivka in Port Saltspray"
Trapped in a seedy port town because an innkeeper is holding her shapeshifting dragon-horse hostage until she can pay all the charges he invented, nomadic warrior Rivka finally has a chance at some decent money when a wealthy but weak man hires her to rescue his fiancée. But she has to think on her feet when she learns there may be more at stake.
"Aviva and the Aliens"
On the night before the royal Passover seder, Aviva has to outsmart the aliens who abducted her to cook for them because they had grown sick of their spaceship's food replicators. Will she get home before Queen Shulamit wakes up and panics from her absence?

Cover art by Rebecca Schauer and Jane Dominguez

Dedicated to Kate the Great
and to the memory of Dame Agatha Christie,
whose greatness I can never touch,
but it sure was fun to try!

♫

Chapter 1: Jewels

Queen Shulamit carefully studied the two necklaces before her. Below the throne platform, the men who had brought them eyed her nervously, occasionally glancing with scorn in each other's direction. She did her best to ignore the tension in front of her and concentrated on her work. It was obvious that each of the jewelers had selected his necklace to appeal to her favorite colors, but she wasn't about to let that influence her decision, and it irritated her that they were trying to manipulate her so cheaply. Would they have done the same for her late father, had they been quibbling over something men wore instead of jewelry? *Probably not, but moving on...* she thought as she fingered the clasp on the lilac-jade beads, her arms bent gingerly around the infant princess sleeping wrapped to her chest. The beads, predictably, matched the wrap.

The clasp opened and closed easily, and when she tugged on the closed loop, it did not come undone. "Good craftsmanship," she commented in an undertone. Naomi would have been with her in the sling anyway, but it was awfully useful to be able to declare that all those presenting their cases for arbitration before the queen must speak calmly and softly if the princess was present, and especially if the princess was sleeping.

"Thank you very much, Your Majesty," said one of the men, his face glowing with pride. His name was Gershom.

The other one, Zev, spoke on top of him. "We're both good craftsmen, but that's not the issue. That's my design! He—"

"She wasn't saying anything about *your* craftsmanship," Gershom interjected pointedly.

"Well, let's see." The queen examined the other necklace, a circlet with a butterfly made from pink gemstones. The clasp seemed identical to the first one, just as strong and just as easy to open and close. "It's the same as the other."

1

"That's the wrong way 'round!" Zev protested. His tone had risen slightly in his agitation, and from behind the queen, a huge figure with well-sculpted muscles shifted slightly. The jeweler was cowed back into a baby-appropriate tone of voice. "It's not the same as his; his is the same as mine. I invented that clasp. I'd been working on it on and off for years, and it's based on an idea my wife had before she died."

"I'm sorry about your wife, but maybe if it hadn't taken you so long to develop her design, I wouldn't have come up with it independently first," commented the jeweler of the jade beads.

"That's ridiculous! I don't know how you did it, but you got into my workshop and—"

"How? When? Your landlady has the keys," said Gershom. "Why would she give them to anyone but you—especially to me! She knows we hate each other."

"Then you broke in," retorted Zev.

"And left no evidence?"

"Then you bribed her."

"You know that's ridiculous," said Gershom. "She's been trying to marry you ever since you rented out the workshop."

Zev opened and closed his mouth rapidly like a dying fish. "That doesn't mean she can't suddenly change her mind about who she'd rather throw herself at!"

"Oh, please!"

"You're a dirty liar, Gershom! You knew my necklaces were going to wipe yours off the map next year with that clasp, and you found some way, I don't know how—"

A dissonant wail pierced the air. "Okay, folks, we're done for now." Shulamit stood, bouncing her fussing infant slightly as she

2

cradled her to her chest. "Leave the evidence with me, and the guards will let you know when I need you again."

"But—!" each man yelled.

She smiled at them as if oblivious, stepping down from the platform of the throne. "You've made your cases. We'll investigate it thoroughly. Don't worry! Peace." It was a dismissal.

The hulking figure in brown leather had stepped out from behind the throne and was approaching the two jewelers. Eyeing the guard uneasily, they both hurried for the doorway on the far side of the room.

When they had gone, the queen turned to the captain of her guard. "That could have gone on all day."

"Put them in a pit and sell tickets," the guard suggested flippantly in a heavy accent. "*Nu*? Did the *schmendrick* on the right steal the other one's... whatever it was?"

"Shhhh, my love," Shulamit cooed to the baby. Then she looked back up. "I'm going to have to think about it. It seems like there's a pretty good motivation for the witness to stay loyal to her tenant, and there's no evidence of a break-in. But somehow... Rivka, I just don't think Zev was lying."

"Which one was that?"

"The pink necklace."

"The accuser."

"Yeah. I almost wonder, I mean, do you think maybe *magic* is involved, somehow?"

Rivka shrugged. "For that, you have to talk to Isaac."

Naomi had stopped crying and was now squirming around and moving her head, trying to find new things to look at. "Has Aviva gone to market yet?" Shulamit asked. "I need to get out of this room. And I think Naomi's bored too."

"I think she's going to go this afternoon, so we can probably come along."

"Go find Isaac and we'll all go together," said Shulamit. "And put these somewhere safe." She deposited the two necklaces into Rivka's waiting hands and then aimed herself at the entrance, where the glorious light of the outdoors beckoned invitingly.

♫

Behind a table in the marketplace, piled high with fruit, stood a middle-aged woman and a young man. The woman was calling out to all the passersby about how their fruit juice was fresh and delicious and tasted like treasure. The young man was busily smashing fruit into a bowl with a pestle, picking out seeds and rinds with his other hand.

During a slow moment, the hawker bent her head toward her companion. "Oh, good, you're really getting the hang of it."

The other one looked up at her through sweat-drenched eyelashes. "This is hard work and we've been at it for hours!"

"This is what we do," said the woman proudly. "I told your father I'd look after you and get you straightened out."

"Mmmmmggnn," grunted the man, who was her nephew.

"Decent work, that's all you needed," she continued cheerfully. "Oh, hey, Caleb, look! Over there, it's the queen and her guards! See, isn't it much more exciting here than in Ir Ilan?"

"Queen Shulamit?" Caleb looked up from his thousandth bowl of juice. He saw a rather ordinary-looking woman, very short and very slender, with a plain face and heavy eyebrows. Her skin was a smooth medium brown like the rest of her countrymen, and her thick black hair was braided tightly into two pigtails that were

4

coiled together behind her head. Strange jewels that complemented her light yellow dress shone from her ears and throat. "She looks just like she does on the money. I thought maybe they'd messed up the portrait, but..."

"Royal blood doesn't make you pretty," his aunt reminded him. "And she's a decent person. She's in the marketplace all the time, but she never expects us to drop whatever we're doing and cater to her. Not like some people who don't even have a quarter of her power. I guess," she added as she picked up another mortar and began to help with the juicing, "she has nothing to prove."

"Who's the pretty one?" Next to the queen, a beauty with messy hair piled on top of her head and held in place by two sticks chattered merrily, peering in and out of stalls with sharp-looking eyes. She was comfortably built with curvaceous hips and a large bosom that he couldn't help but stare at for a moment.

"Oh, that's Aviva. She's the queen's personal chef and constant companion. Those two are never apart for very long."

"You'd think the queen would be afraid to have such a pretty companion. Isn't she afraid Aviva's going to steal her prince consort?"

"He lives somewhere else on a vineyard," she replied vaguely.

"Why are their guards foreign?"

"I don't know."

"Are they brothers? They look similar."

"No, they don't. You're just saying that because they're not Perachi."

Caleb squinted at them curiously. They were both very broad and very tall, and their skin was a much lighter gold than a native Perachi's. Both of the guards had hair the color of brass—one long and messy and past his shoulders, the other cropped short, as

5

was the faint beard and mustache that ringed his mouth. Strangest of all, the one with long hair wore a cloth mask covering the bottom half of his face. "They look like something out of a legend," he murmured.

"The one with the mask is Captain Riv," said Caleb's aunt, "and the older one holding the baby princess is Isaac, the wizard."

Suddenly, a pair of steel-blue eyes was on him. The guard had heard his name. He lifted a pointed eyebrow at the juice stand, and Caleb and his aunt both flushed. "Juice for the queen?" she offered.

Shulamit stepped forward, surveying the booth with searching eyes. Whatever she was looking for apparently satisfied her, so she nodded quickly. "Does anyone else want?"

"We'll share one," said the one called Isaac, who had been conferring with his compatriot. His voice was exceedingly deep and reminded Caleb of when he and his friends back in Ir Ilan had amused themselves calling out into a cave to hear their voices echoed and magnified. Caleb also noticed an accent, but that made sense if they were foreign.

"I can't get over this big, tall guard carrying around a baby princess," Caleb whispered as they prepared the beverages.

"Well, he's not your ordinary man," explained his aunt. "Like I was trying to tell you, they're not brothers." And then she made an awkward face that Caleb finally understood.

"*Ooohhhhh*, okay! Wow, really? I wasn't expecting that. They look like such big heroes." Caleb was staring at the visible biceps on both men, the height that far exceeded his own, and the statuesque posture.

"They are! It doesn't get in the way. Honestly, think about it— why should it?"

6

Caleb eyed them suspiciously. If they were that big and powerful, and they both liked other men, he hoped they wouldn't notice him. He supposed he could take care of himself in a fight against one or even two other Perachis, but these two with their northern genes—huge! He shuddered.

Shulamit accepted the drinks and handed one to Captain Riv. Then with her free hand, she fished some coins out of her pocket.

The owner of the stall held up her hand. "Majesty, you come here so often and I'm still grateful for those stirring words you spoke on Rosh Hashanah. This one's on me."

"Thank you so much! But that's next month—*oh*, you mean last year." The queen smiled awkwardly with half her face, with a combination of warmth and embarrassment in her eyes. "Thank you. That's very sweet of you—" she began, but was suddenly interrupted by a commotion at the back of the stall.

"Hey!" Auntie Juice whirled around as a thin figure slipped swiftly through the crates of fruit. Caleb could see a pair of hands desperately holding on to as many starfruits as could fit. "Get him!"

Caleb sprang up and tried to catch the little thief, but he was tired after his first day of honest work in a year, and the starfruit thief was gone before he could do anything. "Do you want me to go after him?"

His aunt let out a noise like a dog snoring. "Micah is such a pain in my rear end. He's just a kid, but he's always up in everyone's stock; lives on the street—"

"Please," interrupted a female voice, and they both looked back at the queen, having temporarily forgotten her presence. "Take my coins; let it pay for what he took today."

"Well... okay. Thank you, Your Majesty."

7

Caleb, behind his aunt, studied the queen. Well, of course she could afford to be so generous, with all those jewels she was wearing! He wondered what they were; he'd never seen pale yellow gems before. But they matched her dress perfectly. *She's probably wealthy enough that she's got jewels to match any color dress she ever wears*, he mused as he watched her walk away sipping her drink.

His aunt gave him a sharp look, and he hastened for a topic of discussion that would prove he wasn't thinking about the queen's riches. "So one of those men was a wizard?"

"Isaac," said Auntie Juice. "I've never seen it happen, but they say he can turn into a serpent."

"But she trusts him enough to keep him so close."

"Oh yes, he and Queen Shulamit are very close. I don't know if you remember, but she was only twenty when her father died. Isaac stepped in and was there for her, and now he's pretty much got free run of the palace. More than a guard, even—like a second father."

"Must be a good life for him," said Caleb, picking up the pestle to return to what seemed like endless work.

Chapter 2: The Woman with the Violin

It was late afternoon, and Shulamit had dozed off, cuddled into Aviva's soft, fleshy side. The baby was fast asleep on Aviva's chest, and the whole family was so comfortable that it took at least a minute before Shulamit realized that someone was calling her name.

Or at least, one very special *pet* name.

"*Malkeleh*! Aviiiivaleh... come on, wake up so we have enough time to get to the recital."

"I'm up," said Shulamit with her eyes closed. Then she put on her mental crown and forced herself out of bed. "Mhmm," she grunted to Rivka, who was pacing around the room like a caged lion. "What state is my hair in?"

"Black," said Rivka, who never paid much attention to her own wild blonde mane, as long as it wasn't caught in something.

"Very funny." Shulamit undid one of her braids and with busy fingers started resurrecting it.

Aviva stirred on the bed and then sat up, Naomi in her arms. "She probably needs to eat again before you give her to my mother."

"Yeah, the recital should be close to an hour, and then there's travel time. Just let me do this other braid."

"I'll do it for you." A flirtatious look came into Aviva's face, still veiled in drowsiness. "C'mere, you."

Shulamit sat back down and leaned the unkempt side of her head towards Aviva. Naomi woke up and started fussing, and Aviva passed her over so that she could nurse.

9

Before too long, they were standing at the door to the room where Aviva's parents, Leah and Ben, made their home. Ben, who also sold his clothing at the marketplace, was Shulamit's official royal tailor, and their living quarters were large enough to double as a fitting room. Ben was still at market, but Leah's face lit up when she saw them, and she straightened in the chair where she'd been sitting to read. She didn't get up, because then she could use both arms to reach for the baby instead of having one hand occupied by her cane.

"How's my sweetest princess?" Leah cooed as Shulamit placed Naomi into her arms.

"In case she wants," Aviva explained as she handed over a small parcel containing mashed banana.

"Let's see if it goes in her mouth this time instead of all over her face!" Leah's eyes were twinkling.

"It's a beauty aid, haven't you heard?" Shulamit had a sarcastic side. "Latest thing from Imbrio."

Aviva stuck out her tongue.

They met Rivka in the palace courtyard. Isaac was with her, already in his dragon form, and they all eagerly climbed aboard his vast back. Shulamit nestled into Aviva's strong, squishy arms and reveled in the feeling of the wind whipping around her face as they soared into the sky.

Over the prosperous bustle of Home City they flew. Shulamit, as she always did, admired the gleaming, clean brightness of the white buildings with their rippled red-tile roofs, separated by broad-leaved banana stands or towering date palms. This was the land over which she'd been given title by her father's untimely death, the people below her as much her responsibility as the child she'd left in Leah's arms back at the palace. She watched them scurrying about as she flew past them and imagined how impressive Isaac must look to them from down there—a great, black-green shape against the long, honeyed rays of a waning afternoon sun, giant wings in the shape of a bat's propelling himself forward.

On the other side of the city, there was a lake at the bottom of a smooth, grassy hill. Some king who had come before her had built a stage at the shore, and there the people of Home City often enjoyed concerts or public events. They brought blankets or chairs and sat on the grass, and if the event was supposed to last a long time, they brought picnic baskets. The recital of Esther of the Singing Hands, however, was only supposed to last an hour, so there were few baskets. But there were still opportunists here and there selling coconuts with the tops lopped off, in case anyone needed a drink.

Shulamit, as queen, was entitled to special seating at the base of the hill, nearest the stage, but Isaac landed at the back of the crowd because there didn't seem to be enough room for him to land any closer. "Except *on* the stage," he pointed out as his feet grasped the ground.

Rivka scrambled off his back and began helping the other two women to the grass. "And then what? They'd make you sing and everyone would hear how magnificent you sound?"

"Flattery will get you everywhere," he replied, his wings sinking back into his now-human shoulder blades. Isaac's voice was very deep and sonorous, but when he was a dragon, there was an echoing, harsh quality to it and some of the sweetness was gone. Shulamit was fascinated by the difference.

Shulamit walked beside Isaac as they made their way through the crowd, continuing the conversation they'd begun during the flight. "So, now that you've heard all the details, what do you think?"

"Well," said Isaac before taking a breath and pausing, "there are a few different forms of magic that someone could use to get into a workshop without anyone finding out. The most obvious one is

11

shapeshifting. Nobody ever notices my lizard form, so if he could turn into a lizard or a bug or a worm, he'd have every advantage."

"Would anyone really spend all that time training just to be able to turn into a worm?" Shulamit made a face.

"Sometime when you're really bored, ask me about Schlomo the Confused. But don't get your hopes up about the jewelers," Isaac was quick to add. "I've been around Gershom enough to know he doesn't have that level of magical training, at least. And that also rules out invisibility, which takes even longer than shapeshifting."

"Aww, that's too bad. That's exactly the kind of thing I was hoping had happened. I mean, not *hoping*, but..." Shulamit played with the ends of her gauzy yellow scarf. "So, what else?"

"You're not going to like the next thing, because it means a lot of problems for the police."

"I guess that means you don't like it, either, because you *are* the police."

"It's possible that someone *with* magical abilities is selling illegal shifting potions to ordinary people."

"That would certainly be fabulous," the little queen said in a biting tone.

"Or illegal mind-control devices," Isaac added. "The landlady— you talked to her?"

Shulamit nodded. "She didn't seem like she was lying or bewitched. But would I even be able to tell if she was bewitched?"

"I don't know," said Isaac. "*I* might be able to tell if it had just happened, but I don't know how much I would perceive if it happened sometime in the past."

"Rrrrgh. That's why this stuff is illegal."

12

"You'll sort it out, *Malkeleh!*" Rivka interjected cheerfully. "You always do."

They bought coconuts from one of the vendors and sat down near the front of the crowd. As Shulamit sipped the sweet water from hers, she listened to the voices of her people around her. Some of them were talking about the performer, Esther of the Singing Hands, who was internationally renowned for her violin playing. She came from Lovely Valley, in the southeast of Perach past the mountain range, and had returned to tour her home country after performing in high court of Imbrio. Apparently, she'd made such a splash there that both the Princess of Imbrio's little son and daughter had demanded to take up violin lessons.

Shulamit, who'd had a raging, awkward crush on Princess Carolina when they were both teenagers, shifted her focus to another conversation on which to eavesdrop.

The other group of people was talking about Liora, Home City's native violin star, and pointed her out among the wealthy in the crowd. Shulamit automatically followed their hands to the tall, thin figure at the end of the row, wearing over her simple black dress a man's coat with a fitted waist and skirt like Isaac's, only where his was silver, hers was a brilliant scarlet. Something red and jeweled held an explosion of thick, curly black hair away from her face, and she gazed out at the lake dispassionately, as if unaware of how many people were talking about her. According to the audience, at least the ones within earshot of Shulamit, Liora and Esther were passionate rivals. Their reputations certainly contrasted; Esther was purported to be sweet and gentle, whereas Liora was legendary for her flamboyance and flirtations.

Liora was sitting with the marquis, which was normal. He was her patron, and some people said he was her lover. He could have been her pet ostrich for all Shulamit cared; she'd found him irritating ever since he'd "helpfully" tried to explain to her how she could thin out her thick eyebrows. They were a connection to her father, and for whose sake did she need to be prettier, anyway?

Servants dressed in blue appeared on either side of the stage and lit torches so that as the sun began to set, people could still see the performance. It was also a signal for the crowd to hush. Then, from the side, a beautiful, plump lady stepped out with her violin tucked under her arm and her bow hanging from one finger. She smiled at the applauding audience, and Shulamit perceived the contradictory emotions of confidence and extreme vulnerability. She was younger than Shulamit had expected; she hadn't realized Esther was only in her early twenties.

Esther lifted her bow to the waiting violin and began.

Shulamit's heart was stirred instantly, and she sidled closer to Aviva and felt her own face split in half smiling as the elegant tones painted the air with rich colors of sound. She had the fleeting idea that her great-grandfather, who had been a renowned musician and had written some of the national tunes, was trying to speak to her through the violin. But—wait—it had belonged to his teacher, not to him. For a moment, she had misremembered the story. And in any case, it was unfair to take the credit away from this marvelous young woman who clearly had the talent to create magic with her fingers as real as any spell of Isaac's.

This was why they called her Esther of the Singing Hands.

At the end of the performance, after the torrent of cheers and applause, Isaac and Rivka made the way clear for Shulamit to visit with Esther behind the stage so that she could tell her how much she'd enjoyed herself. When she rounded the corner behind the huge boulders that flanked the stage, she saw the violinist surrounded by other admirers, but none so near as the thin but fit young man who hovered protectively and never left her side. He wore his bushy hair in a low ponytail that hung past his shoulders, and she took breaks every so often from greeting her fans to gaze at him with an expression of pure molasses.

A very large man in every dimension was complimenting her profusely, and when he turned to go, Shulamit noticed a look of scorn in the eyes of the violinist's suitor. He barely waited until the large man had walked out of earshot before saying something to Esther that darkened her expression into a pout. As Shulamit drew closer, she heard Esther saying, "That's mean. And anyway, those were such nice things he said!"

"I've come to say nice things too," Shulamit spoke up.

Esther and the man both bowed when they noticed the queen. "Your Majesty! I'm so glad to meet you!" Esther exclaimed. "The Princess of Imbrio talked about you."

Caught in the unexpected awkwardness, Shulamit blinked rapidly several times before Isaac jumped in and saved her. "Magnificent performance. Such good programming too—not too many of the same style one right after the other."

"Your hands sang *and* danced," Aviva agreed gleefully.

"Thank you for making Perach proud," said Shulamit, who had found her words thanks to the supportive rescue from her loved ones. "I don't know how much longer you're staying in Home City, but I'd love to have you come to the palace and play for my daughter. She's only six months old, but I bet she'd love it!"

"Oh, Your Majesty! That would be really meaningful for me," said Esther. "My very first audience, when I was a small child, was my baby sisters."

"See?" said Shulamit, smiling her usual half-smile. "Just like home!"

"I know we'll be here another few days at least," Esther continued.

"The only fixed thing on her calendar is tonight's party at the inn." It was the young man, speaking to the queen for the first time.

"Oh! I'm sorry, Your Majesty. I forgot to introduce Eli. He's—"

15

"Eli. I'm her fiancé. I'm studying law." He looked at Esther convivially.

"—my boyfriend from back home," Esther finished even though he had spoken on top of her. She grinned and chuckled at him affectionately.

"Honored to meet you, Majesty!" said Eli.

"Pleased to meet you. And this is Aviva, and my guards, Isaac and Riv." Shulamit gestured behind her.

"Yes, the legendary northerners," said Eli, looking them over.

"So you're going to a party later?" Shulamit asked.

Esther opened her mouth, but Eli was already talking. "Yes, the innkeeper insisted on it."

"He's so proud of having me stay there," Esther said with an embarrassed smile. "It's not a very big party."

"I'm sure he'd be honored if you attended," said Eli to the queen.

"Thank you," said Shulamit, "but I probably won't, sorry. I have to go home and make sure the princess gets fed." The part she wasn't explaining to a stranger was that it was troublesome for her to eat food far from the safety of Aviva's kitchen because of her peculiar problems digesting wheat or poultry. Most people didn't believe her and thought she was just claiming special ailments out of royal vanity, but then, she hadn't thrown up all over most people.

As Shulamit peeled away from the couple, she noticed Aviva ending a conversation with the large man who'd preceded her at the receiving line. "Who was that?"

"Oh, we were talking about the market," said Aviva, linking hands with her. "I said I thought he looked familiar, and he said

16

he'd just come to town and set up at market last week, selling musical instruments."

"Does he like it here?"

"Seems to! He travels around, though. More of a hummingbird than a hibiscus."

They'd waited long enough for the crowd to disperse, so Isaac didn't mind transforming right on the stage. With the most important ladies in his life ensconced safely on his back, he took off into the night sky.

Several hours later, Shulamit sat in Aviva's kitchen, once again nursing Naomi as the four of them digested their dinner. "She did well with that avocado," she commented.

"If by 'did well,' you mean she got enough in her mouth to count as eating," said Rivka, "because there was on her face enough green that I am thinking she could be a dragon like him!"

"Maybe someday she'll follow in his footsteps." Shulamit looked down at the wide-eyed, contented little creature.

♫

Meanwhile, far away across the city in the inn near the lake, Esther of the Singing Hands was returning to her room after the party. She crossed the inner courtyard, walking slowly in the dark, and unlocked the door. In the light of the candle that she sat down on the bedside table, she scanned the room with quickly widening eyes. Where was her violin?

She paced around the bed, craning her head here and there and even stooping to the floor to look under it. Nothing. "Eli!" she called out, wondering if he'd hear her. His room faced the outside, the street, instead of the inner courtyard. "Eli, I need you!"

Circling the room over and over, she kept looking, unable to believe the evidence of her own eyes. Somehow Eli had heard her and appeared in the doorway. "What's the matter?"

"Where's my violin?"

"Did you leave it at the lake?"

"No! When have I ever done anything like that?"

"Maybe you were distracted from meeting the queen."

"No, I remember putting it just there, on the floor by the bed," Esther murmured, her words coming out rapid-fire, "so that if anything happened in the night I'd be able to grab it on my way out of the room. I remember putting it just by that knothole in the floor; I remember thinking how funny it was that it looked like a cat's head." Her voice grew louder. "There's hardly anything in this room—nowhere else it could be. Do you see it? I don't see it!"

Someone else came to the doorway, and Eli spoke with them under his breath. Esther continued to wheel around the room, hoping that the next time she rounded the bed, it would be there, and all this would be a funny nightmare they'd laugh about later.

"What's happened?" said the innkeeper. There were servants with him, as well as curious guests who'd been in the courtyard and were attracted by the commotion.

"Her violin's gone missing," Eli explained in an even tone.

"What? In my inn?"

"The door was locked," Esther exclaimed.

"The lock's been picked," one of the servants pointed out.

"What?" Heat suffused Esther's face, and her heart sank into her stomach and made her feel sick.

18

"I suppose it's been stolen," said Eli.

"You two, go summon the queen. She's good at this sort of thing." Esther heard the innkeeper talking to his servants from what seemed like a thousand miles away as she sank down upon the bed, uncontrollably sobbing.

Chapter 3: Esther of the Empty Hands

"Here, Esther, drink this."

"Whaa?" What came out of her mouth sounded more like the plaintive moan of an infant than any noise an adult had a right to make. Esther picked herself up from the tearstained arms where she'd been mushing her face and saw that Eli was handing her a cup.

"Drink the tea. Calm you down. Please?"

She leaned back into the comfort of his familiar embrace and accepted the offering.

"The queen is in the lounge," said the innkeeper, who was standing close to the door. Everybody else had gone. "Please come and talk to her. She needs to know what it looks like."

"You haven't found it?" Esther slowly rose from the bed and groped around for her new blue scarf that had been draped modestly around her bare shoulders during the after-concert party. It had come undone during her crying fit.

"I'm afraid not," said the innkeeper.

"No," said Eli, shaking his head. They spoke at the same time.

Esther peered around the room, feeling as if surely, *surely* this must be a nightmare. She'd come out of a bed, right? So there was a chance that if she went back to it, she could open her eyes again and everything would be just as it should be, with her fiddle by her side, ready to come to life under her loving fingers?

Instead, Eli took her hand and led her outside into the darkness of the outdoor inner courtyard, farther into the night.

20

Coming back to the inn's lounge after the violin's disappearance left *nightmare, nightmare, nightmare* echoing in Esther's head in steady, slow beats. Here she'd spent the past few hours, happily talking with the innkeeper's guests and raking in the compliments over a light dinner. The table was still there, but cleared; the potted lime trees were perched in the corners as before. She'd been content here so recently. Now she was devastated.

Servants had brought in a fresh set of candles, and in their flickering light she once again beheld the Queen of Perach. There was a graveness in the small woman's face, and behind her, her two foreign bodyguards loomed in the shadows.

"Your Majesty—again, thank you—thank you so much for coming out here so late," the innkeeper gushed with his head down.

"It's best to check these things out as soon as possible," said Queen Shulamit, "right after they happen, to see things as they are."

"How did you get here so quickly?" Eli hovered near Esther protectively, one hand near the small of her back. "And here with no trace of the servants who sent for you."

"As you may have heard, I have a dragon," was the queen's answer.

"Please, Majesty," Esther said in a choked voice. "It's got to be somewhere."

"A priceless violin," mused the unmasked guard in a deep voice. "Lots of people would want that somewhere to be *their* somewhere."

"What does it look like?" asked Queen Shulamit. "I was at your concert, but I wasn't looking at it up close."

"The wood is dark brown," said Esther, "and the body is large so that the sound is... is fabulous." She never thought she'd ever had

21

to describe it like this, her—body part, her voice, the way her soul spoke to the world. Surely it wasn't a curved container of dark wood with holes in the top for resonance and a spiraling scroll where the pegs stuck out. How prosaic! One might as well say one's boyfriend was a collection of meat and hair.

"When did you notice it missing?"

"I went back to my room at the end of the party, and the first thing I noticed was that it wasn't there," said Esther. "The case is hard to miss—"

"Oh, so it was in a case?"

"Yes, Majesty. A wooden case, painted with sparkly butterflies. Big, lopsided, sparkly butterflies." Esther grinned despite herself. "When my parents bought it for me, my baby sisters painted the case to surprise me, and to congratulate me. My mother was angry but, you know? I liked it! It looks silly, but it reminds me of them and how much they support me."

"So the case was gone? Not just empty and lying there?"

"Exactly. Completely gone." Esther closed her eyes, pressing the burning lids together so that she wouldn't do something silly like cry in front of the queen.

She needn't have worried. A gentle hand had reached for hers. "I'm going to do what I can." Esther opened her eyes to see the queen turn to the innkeeper. "Who was at the party?"

"Well," began the innkeeper, licking his lips, "Esther and this Eli fellow... the marquis, of course, with Liora, and that instrument-selling man. All music people."

"Is the instrument seller staying here?"

"Yes, Majesty. But he's gone off with Liora back to the marquis' manor to look at something."

"Everyone will be summoned to the palace in the morning so that I can hear what they all have to say." The queen paced around the room and then looked out into the inner courtyard. "The only way into that courtyard is through this lounge, right?"

"Yes, Majesty."

"Was anyone sitting in the courtyard during the party?"

"There was a rabbi from out of town who's staying here, and some older ladies having an argument... at least, that's what it looked like."

"Then hopefully one of them saw whoever it was lurking near the door to Esther's room."

Esther was able to detach a little bit, now that the conversation had drifted from the specifics of the stolen object. It was almost as though it had nothing to do with her and she could pretend everything was normal. But the tears came back when the queen asked to see her room. "Yes... yes, I'll show you where it was."

Just as they were leaving, there was a scuffle near the front door of the lounge, the one that opened out to the street. A servant was holding a thin figure by the shoulder as he roughly dragged him into the room. He deposited him in front of the innkeeper, who said, "There's your thief," through scowling lips.

"What? It's just tea from the kitchen," said the boy, who looked as though he was only ten or eleven but seemed a little more mature. Esther wondered if living on the street had brought him to adulthood prematurely, or at least bits of it. "They *gave* it to me."

"Did they?" The innkeeper looked the boy over. Esther did as well and saw a figure so thin it reminded her of her own bow, draped in rags. The legs of his pants weren't the same lengths, so tattered had they grown, and even in candlelight his feet were among the dirtiest she'd ever seen. "Tea or no tea, we're not worried about that right now. Were you in the inner courtyard tonight? Did you take this woman's violin?"

"Oh, sure, I just walked in through your fancy fat-cat party, into the courtyard, and took whatever I wanted, and nobody saw me." The boy scowled. "'Cause I got magical powers." There was sarcasm and contempt dripping from his voice. It seemed oddly hardened for a child so young.

"Shut your mouth, boy," the innkeeper snapped. "Majesty, have your guards arrest this little troublemaker and your problem will be solved. And so will mine."

"Is there any other way into the courtyard besides this lounge?" the queen asked the innkeeper.

"Well, no."

"Then I don't see how it could have been him," said Queen Shulamit.

The innkeeper was forced to admit that she had a point. "He's still trouble."

"Is that his name?"

"His name is Micah," the innkeeper growled.

"I want to talk to him in the morning, with the rest of them," said the queen, "but I'm not arresting him now because he couldn't have stolen Esther's violin or her spare hair ornaments or anything else that was in her private room."

"You can talk to me when you find me!" And with that, the scamp darted out again into the street.

The guard with the mask, confidently tossing his head, said something in a guttural foreign tongue to the other guard, who responded with a flirtatious half-smile, baffling Esther. As for the queen, she seemed nonplussed by Micah's escape. Esther figured she had dismissed him as a threat, which made sense—what would a starving child, even a rude one, need with a priceless violin anyway?

The thought suddenly flashed into her mind that even a starving child—*especially* a starving child—can sell his honor for money to buy food and safety, and there had been an instrument dealer at their party...

Esther didn't want him to have anything to do with it. He'd seemed like such a nice man, and she'd enjoyed talking with him! But he still made her feel uneasy, and she hadn't been able to explain why. Had her heart been trying to tell her something?

Badly wishing she had her violin still so she could lose herself in simple folk tunes and *think*, she led the queen to the location of the theft.

Chapter 4: Mother Justice

"Bouncy bouncy frog says hop hop!" It was morning, and Shulamit was sitting on her throne with her daughter facing her on her lap. Naomi was giggling as her mother danced her up and down, her little face radiant with the sheer joy of being alive. "Frog frog *frog!*"

"Such dignified wisdom from the throne of Perach," Rivka joked gently.

Shulamit stuck out her tongue. "I'll have to act regal soon enough. Go see if everyone's done being checked for weapons." She leaned Naomi forward and planted a big kiss on her forehead. "Froggie!"

Rivka crossed the empty throne room and opened one of the doors at the far end. Meanwhile, Naomi pawed at Shulamit's chest. She quickly arranged herself, pulling aside a convenient flap in the top of her elaborate papaya-orange dress. Naomi was latched by the time Rivka reappeared. "Do I look dignified yet?"

"Sitting there with her nursing, with that solemn face, you look like Mother Justice."

Shulamit smirked. "I like that. It's been a long time since this country's seen a queen on the throne, and that includes things like nursing." Shulamit had succeeded her father, grandfather, and great-grandfather in rule; there had not been a woman born as the first or only royal child in several generations.

"They're certainly not about to forget a woman leads this country with you sitting there like that," said Rivka approvingly. "Tivon's almost ready to send in the witnesses."

"Good. How's that kid, after what he put you through this morning?"

"Micah?" Rivka strode back across the room and took up her usual position behind Shulamit's throne. "Trying to act tough, but he seemed glad for a full meal."

"That's Aviva for you." Shulamit felt a current of pleasant warmth trickle across her mind at the thought. Then she firmed up her expression. "I'm ready when they are."

The first person to come in was the instrument seller whom Shulamit had seen complimenting Esther after her performance the previous night. He was tall, and broad, and very fat, and he seemed nonthreatening and kind. Shulamit studied his appearance, trying to parse his ethnicity. His skin was the same medium brown as her own and that of her people, but his hair was thick and coarse and pulled into the rough locks that looked like braids but weren't, like the people to the south whose skin was darker.

He knelt when he reached the throne.

"Peace," said Shulamit solemnly, "and good morning."

"Good morning, Your Majesty."

"What's your name?"

"Tzuriel ben Kofi, Majesty. I'm a dealer of musical instruments and supplies."

"Kofi?" She didn't know the name.

"My father is a fisherman on the Sugar Coast," he explained.

Shulamit nodded. Now his hair made sense. "Rise, Tzuriel." He obeyed. "Did you grow up in Perach or down south?" These things had nothing to do with Esther's violin, but people were often nervous in situations like this, both because of her rank and because of the association with a crime, so she liked to get them conversing to settle their stomachs.

27

"Down South—though I'd been to Perach many times to visit my mother's family."

"And now you travel around selling your wares. How do you like Home City?"

"Magnificent, Majesty. The capital seems to be doing well economically, and you've all taken that prosperity and used it to invest in culture."

"That's thanks to our farmers," said Shulamit. "The land is full of riches, but without those who would work for them, we'd be unable to afford things like last night's concert. I saw many of them on the hill last night, and I was glad they were enjoying the results of their labors."

"Fantastic concert!" Tzuriel agreed. "I'd seen Esther before, but she's gotten even better."

"Did you know her before last night?"

"No. I never went backstage until this time."

"Do you know anything about her violin?"

"It's a historical treasure. They say it belonged to King Asher's music teacher. I was trying to get a look at it last night, but it never seemed like the right time to ask."

"So you never got to study it up close?"

"No, Majesty."

"Do you know where it is now?"

"I would assume in Esther's room someplace—or else with the innkeeper's security? I don't know if she leaves her fiddle with the staff when she travels."

"So nobody's told you about the theft."

28

Tzuriel's mild expression shifted into shocked dismay. "What? Is that what this is about?"

"Did you have anything to do with it?"

"Your Majesty, I may be an outsider, but I'm an honest man. You're welcome to inspect my entire stock. There's nothing there that doesn't belong." He looked more hurt than angry.

"Please don't take it personally," said Shulamit, who hated causing unpleasantness. "I have to talk to everybody who was there last night."

"Yes, I know." Tzuriel looked over at Rivka, then at the floor.

"How long was the party in the inn?"

"About two hours."

"Who was there?"

"Esther and that man from her hometown, the local fiddler and her patron, and the innkeeper."

"Did anyone else enter at any time?"

"Servants came to bring us food and refill our drinks. They also took away the plates."

"Did they come from the outside or from the courtyard?"

"From the courtyard. I think the kitchen is on the other side." He smiled self-consciously. "The entrance was behind me, and I had to move a little every time someone wanted to go outside that way, so I noticed people going in or out."

"Good, that'll be important. What about people from the party?"

"I remember the rich man—what is he, a marquis?—going out a few times. But he went out the front door. Esther went to her room at one point, and that was past me—her friend went to his

29

own room a few times, but that would have been out the front door."

"What about Liora?"

"The other fiddler? She didn't leave the room at all until we all left together."

"And the innkeeper?"

"No, he didn't leave that way, either. Only out the front. Also, I did leave myself out the front entrance at one point—just to—you know."

"Just out the front, though."

"That's right."

"Thank you for your help. If you like, there's some brunch waiting in the other room. And please don't leave town until we sort this all out."

The next person to be shown in was the innkeeper. His face was a map of anxiety. "Majesty, please promise me you'll help us. People are glaring at me in the street."

"Why would they do that?"

"No man wants his inn to be thought of as a place where guests have priceless possessions stolen!"

"I'll get to justice, don't worry." Then she flashed him a look that was an attempt at one of Isaac's faces, intimidating confidence mixed with smug serenity. After all, justice would be done even if it meant that the innkeeper *was* guilty. The expression seemed to work, and his eyelids fluttered rapidly with unease. "I have a few questions about your inn first."

"Anything."

"Is there a way into the courtyard besides through the lounge?"

"No, it's all solid wall."

"So nobody could leave the lounge by the front door and then get back into the courtyard some other way?"

"No, Majesty."

"It's either one of your guests or one of your servants," Shulamit pointed out. "I'm sorry."

"But the street kid—"

"Don't worry, I'm going to question him. As a witness. Unless you can explain to me how he got inside the courtyard and into Esther's room without being noticed."

"Is this compassion? Why not have some compassion for me?"

"I'm not talking about compassion. Until you can prove to me that he walked through the wall, I can't see how he would have gotten in."

Several disagreeable moments later, she'd gotten everything she needed from the innkeeper and sent him away to grumble over his brunch.

"Who's next?"

The guards let in one of the inn's guests, a rabbi who'd been sitting in the courtyard all night, very near to Esther's door. "You're traveling through Home City?

"Yes, Majesty. I'm writing a book. I often sit outside for hours, thinking of what I'm going to write next. That's why I was in the courtyard until long past sundown."

"What's your book about?"

"What if God—God Himself!—came down to His people in human form, taking a different life every day for an entire week?

Would it change His perspective, or the way He governs our fate?"

"Sounds like a topic with full potential for philosophy," said the queen. "Is God ever a young mother with a female companion?"

"What?"

"Never mind. So you were in the courtyard the entire evening?"

"Yes, Majesty."

"Did you see anyone enter the room with the blue door, in the far back corner?"

"Yes, I did, a pretty young thing with a full figure."

"Is she here outside this room?"

"Yes, with a gentleman friend, from the way they were acting."

"Did anyone else go near the room at any time?"

"I didn't see anyone else."

Neither did any of the other witnesses in the courtyard. The two older women having an argument whom the innkeeper had mentioned the previous night turned out to be the juice seller from the marketplace and an old friend of hers who was visiting on her way to the Sugar Coast for a spa treatment, and they hadn't seen anything suspicious, either.

"What was the argument about?" Shulamit asked the juice seller.

"Oh, well!" Aunt Juice threw up her hands. "She was saying I was a pushover for taking in my nephew from Ir Ilan. You must have seen him yesterday at the stall—you remember?"

Shulamit murmured in assent.

"He was running with a pretty rough crowd back home, but his parents weren't making him work hard enough. Don't tell them I said that," Aunt Juice added quickly. "They're the ones who are too soft. But I knew if I brought Caleb home with me, I could straighten him out with some good, honest work."

"Was your nephew anywhere near the inn last night?"

"No, he was at my place," said the juice seller. "I set him to work cleaning out my back deck. Keep him busy and out of trouble."

"How's the deck?"

"A lot tidier!" Aunt Juice puffed herself up triumphantly.

Micah was next. He didn't kneel, but Shulamit didn't mind. She studied him from her royal perch, Naomi now sleeping against her breast. "They said your name is Micah."

"It is."

"Do you have any family?"

"Somewhere."

"I know you weren't in the courtyard, because someone would have seen you," said Shulamit, "but do you know anything about Esther's violin?"

"Didn't take anything from her." Micah shifted around, not making eye contact.

"Did anybody give you money to keep quiet?"

"What? Nobody gave me *squat*."

"Aviva gave you breakfast."

Micah looked down. "Yeah. She's nice."

"Did you see anything last night, when you were hanging around the inn?"

"The kitchen people gave me cold falafel and a mug of tea. I wasn't in the courtyard."

Shulamit jumped on a hunch. "Do you feel safer in boy's clothes, since you're on the street?"

"I *am* a boy!" Micah glared at her.

"Girls can be really strong too."

"You don't know *anything*!" Micah shouted, and ran from the room.

Rivka looked at Shulamit as if expecting an order, but Shulamit lifted her hand. "Let him go. I'm done with him for now, anyway."

"What was all that about?" asked Rivka.

"Micah's cross-dressing like you."

"I tracked him all morning and I can tell you one thing—Micah's not like me," said Rivka. "With him, it's something different."

Chapter 5: Liora and the Marquis

The infant princess squirmed and struggled with her little limbs against the confines of the sling. "I think she's had enough of this. Maybe Leah could take her over to the kitchen-house so she can crawl around in that little 'safe corner.'" Shulamit adjusted her clothing now that Naomi had finished nursing for the moment.

"Maybe she's just tired of all the polite conversation and wants me to leap with my sword—hyeah!—to each one of them. *Did you do it? Where is the violin? Answer!*" Rivka joked.

"We'll get there! I'm just being thorough." Shulamit kissed her baby's forehead. "You never know what little detail could wind up being important later. Although, I wish Isaac were here. It's going to be tedious having to repeat all this to him later, even if it does help me remember."

"He's here," Rivka informed her calmly.

Shulamit lifted an eyebrow. "In that case, *Zayde* Lizard, would you mind taking Naomi to the kitchen? If Aviva's too busy to watch her, see what Leah's up to."

The alert little creature emerged from between the wild locks of Rivka's blonde hair. "It's tempting to watch her myself, but I don't want to miss any of this violin business." He scampered down the front of Rivka's body so that when he transformed there wouldn't be a man over six feet tall sitting on her shoulder.

"Don't worry," Shulamit reassured him as he rose up from the floor in human form. "I won't start without you."

A few minutes later, with Isaac once more safely ensconced somewhere on Rivka's person, the next witness—or suspect— was admitted into the room. "Good morning, Marquis," said Shulamit with a fake smile that looked exactly like the grimace it really was plastered across her face.

35

"Peace, Majesty!" said the marquis, approaching the throne and bowing deeply. "It's such a pleasure to come and visit you."

"Thank you, Marquis. Let's talk about last night. You and Liora were there as the innkeeper's guests, correct?"

"That's right, Majesty."

"Did you know in advance that you'd be going over there after the performance?"

"No, Majesty. Our original plans would have taken us for a dinner out at the Frangipani Table, but naturally I preferred the choice of something more exclusive. Of course, I must endure such things from time to time, as Liora loves the attention... Did you know it's impossible for her even to show her face in the market without being pressed for autographs, or asked musical advice, or even the young men bold enough to pay her intimate compliments? Fortunately, she thrives on their adoration. I suppose it's one of the reasons she's taken so naturally to celebrity."

The marquis would have continued forever, as if the sound of his own voice were a lifesaving tonic. Shulamit jumped in, which made her uncomfortable even though she was the queen—it had never seemed fair to her to expect rules of politeness not to apply just because of the accident of her birth, and even though she knew the marquis was the one being rude, interrupting felt awkward. "Once you got to the inn, did you at any point see Esther's violin?"

"No, not at all. We went straight to dinner, and Esther and that overcooked noodle man of hers joined us once she'd put away her things from the recital. What do you make of him, Majesty? Liora would never waste her time with a man like that—so provincial! Puts his nose in the air just because he's studying law. He's not even an advocate yet, just a student. Still, Esther herself doesn't seem all that sophisticated. Just a simple girl from Lovely Valley who happens to have an unusual talent for music. But that's

36

Lovely Valley for you. When was the last time you were in Lovely Valley? I haven't been in ages, but I don't see the draw—nothing but farmers, really."

"This nation was built on the work of farmers," Shulamit said in a flat voice. This was going nowhere. As badly as she wanted to ream him out and defend her people to this popinjay, she had a job to do, or else her crown—her father's crown, really, which she never wore and which sat on her bedside table instead—meant nothing. "Did you leave the room at all during dinner?"

"You know, Majesty, I've just figured out what your dress reminds me of—a papaya! It's exactly the color of a ripe papaya. Not really pink, but not orange, either—"

"You will respect the queen's questions and stop driveling." Rivka had stepped out from behind the throne and was now standing, muscular arms folded over her chest, directly before the marquis. At five foot eleven, she stood three inches taller than he and broader too—plus, she came with a reputation and several pieces of steel.

"My apologies, Majesty," blurted the marquis hurriedly. "Wh-what was the question?"

"Did you leave the room at all?" Shulamit repeated, shooting a look of thanks to Rivka as the warrior took her place behind the throne once more.

"I—no—I—"

"There was a lot of drinking going on, from what I heard. You really never left?"

"Well, yes, Majesty, but you don't expect me to mention something so delicate to you?"

"I've got a baby," said Shulamit with a knowing smirk. "All of that is old news at this point."

The marquis eventually admitted that he had left the room a few times to relieve himself, but during none of those times did he enter the courtyard. He said he was sure Esther and Eli had both gotten up at one point or another, and that he knew the instrument seller had gone to urinate as well because he had asked him where to go on his way out.

Soon, Shulamit was rid of him, and she breathed a sigh of relief when he and his bald spot had disappeared beyond the door. "How does Liora put up with him?"

"Ask her—she's on her way in."

Liora was tall, and slender, and striking. Shulamit had only seen her from a distance in the past—onstage and, most recently, last night at the performance. This was her first look at the celebrated local up close. Liora's dark hair was clasped back with an ornament and fell in untidy waterfalls down her back, and though her clothing was only a simple dress of filmy dark purple linen, somehow she looked like a goddess in it. It wasn't really a matter of beauty—her face was a bit asymmetrical, perhaps even lopsided. Her carriage, her poise, her confidence—this was what commanded attention. And possibly the hair.

Shulamit felt vaguely uncomfortable, the way she always did when she was attracted to someone who wasn't Aviva, and she stifled a childish impulse to put everything on hold and rush to the kitchen-house.

Well, anyway. The world was full of women and some of them were interesting. "Thank you for coming in this morning," Shulamit began. "I want to ask you some questions about last night."

"Yes, of course," said Liora, blinking several times. "My maid told me—the servants are already gossiping about it. When I first heard the news I was so upset I couldn't eat breakfast. I just kept thinking about what it must be like for her—and what I'd feel like if it happened to me. Poor Esther! She's outside in that room there where we were all waiting, sitting in a corner with that accessory male of hers petting her hair."

Shulamit repressed a snicker at "accessory male," and wondered if that was because Liora saw Eli as far more insignificant than her own marquis—or if it was *exactly* how she felt about her own marquis. "Had you ever met Esther before last night?"

"No, I hadn't—wonderful playing, don't you think?"

"I do," said the queen. "The chatter around town is that you two have a healthy rivalry."

"It's just chatter." Liora dismissed the idea with a casual toss of her head. "Musicians should collaborate, not compete. I'd love to do some duets with her—when she gets her fiddle back, obviously."

"Does it bother you that people say that?"

"I shouldn't let it—bad publicity is still publicity, the marquis always says." But Liora wasn't smiling. "I just don't care for the comparisons of our personalities, which usually follow. I always come out sounding like the evil stepmother in a fairytale. Why can't they just talk about our playing?"

"Because we're women, and our looks and personalities are always under scrutiny." Shulamit realized, when Liora had dropped the word "stepmother," that Liora was significantly older than Esther—not old enough to be her mother, but perhaps by ten years. She wondered what kind of a role that played in the way the public saw the two women.

"True at that, Majesty."

"Tell me about last night."

"The innkeeper saw us at the concert and asked if we're like to come to the private reception for his honored guest," Liora explained. "It was fairly relaxed; there weren't even real courses, just servants bringing communal dishes in and out as they were ready."

"Did you leave the room at all during dinner?"

"No."

"Even to go relieve yourself?"

"I held it," said Liora, pressing her lips together in a mischievous smile. "I didn't want anyone to say anything interesting I might miss!"

You didn't want to miss any opportunity for a compliment? Shulamit wondered, then quickly chastised herself for falling into the trap of reputation. "And did anyone say anything interesting?"

"Oh, it was a pleasant evening. I liked everyone there."

"I understand Tzuriel ben Kofi went back with you to the marquis' manor afterward."

"Oh, yes," said Liora. "Years ago, the marquis won a violin in a—gambling, I don't remember where or what he was playing. But I already have my violin, and I didn't like the new one. Too shrill. I think the—" Here she launched into a lengthy technical hypothesis about the violin's structure.

Shulamit, ever the intellectual, wanted to understand, but she knew she needed a foundation first. She made a mental note to read up on violin acoustics. "So you wanted to sell it to him?"

"Yes, it's not for me, but it's an expensive instrument. I didn't want to just donate it to the music academy. If we sell it, the money can be used to buy several cheaper ones for the students."

"Did he decide to buy it?"

Liora sighed heavily. "It didn't work out. Too expensive for what he can unload easily. He carries nice, serviceable, middle-class

40

stock. This ridiculous little box, tinny as it is, seems to be somewhat valuable just because of its age."

"You could have taken less money."

"It's not just up to me."

"Did Tzuriel go back to his room at all before coming home with you?"

"I don't remember, really. I know he left once during dinner." Liora paused dramatically. "I keep thinking this has to be some kind of mistake. That violin was just *too valuable to steal.*"

"How's that again?"

"Well, think about it—even the person in the best position to fence something like that—Mr. Ben Kofi, sweet as he seems— even he'd have to leave the country to be able to sell it without being found out."

"That's true, at this point."

"That's why I keep thinking it must all be a mistake—someone took it without realizing how valuable it was—one of the servants at the inn, or someone else who snuck in somehow."

"Unless the motive wasn't about money."

"What do you mean?"

"I'll let you know if I have more questions," Shulamit said, serenely dismissing her. "Can you please ask Esther to come in next?"

Chapter 6: The Legendary Captain Riv

"Please tell me you've got ideas," Esther begged, the fingertips of both hands lightly touching her lips. "When I woke up this morning, I couldn't remember why I was sad... and then it all came back."

"I'm working on it," said Shulamit. "Let's start at the beginning. Tell me about coming back from the concert."

"Eli and I walked back together, and I left the violin beside the bed, next to the cat-shaped knothole. I rested for a few minutes, and then walked out to the lounge to meet everyone else."

"Do you remember who was in the courtyard when you left your room?"

"Two ladies and an old man."

"Any servants?"

"They were all at the far end, where the kitchen is. They weren't really in the courtyard."

"Did you leave the lounge yourself during dinner?"

"Yes, Eli got me a new scarf in the marketplace yesterday, a gorgeous blue hand-painted silk... I realized I wasn't wearing it, so I went to go get it and show it off."

"You didn't want to wear it during the concert?"

"I can't; it's... my neck..." Her hands fussed in the air near her shoulders.

"I understand. The violin was exactly where you'd left it when you went back for the scarf?"

Esther nodded. "Everything was fine."

"Can you think of anyone who might want to hurt you?"

Blankness suffused Esther's face and she shook it slowly. "People seem to like me," she said in a tiny voice.

"No... obsessed fans following you from city to city?"

"Nothing like that, not yet!" Esther looked embarrassed at the idea.

Shulamit was beginning to understand why her people liked to paint Esther and Liora as innocent and vamp. "What about the others at the party? Did anyone seem especially interested in your instrument? The other violinist, the instrument seller...".

"Oh, of course they all asked me about it, and wanted to see it, but somehow we never quite got to that part. Every time the conversation went there, it seemed to drift away just as quickly. I was relieved, really—I know Liora or even Tzuriel have been around instruments their whole lives and aren't going to break it if they pick it up for thirty seconds to see what it's like, but... there's a protectiveness that goes beyond what my head tells me."

Reminds me of how I feel about Naomi, Shulamit realized. "You can go, for now. Let me know immediately if you hear anything, like a ransom note, or if it turns up again. Or if anything else goes missing."

Eli was the last person Shulamit called in for questioning that morning, and he didn't have much to add to the data, only confirming that, yes, he remembered Esther going back to her room once or twice for feminine reasons like her new scarf, and that he couldn't really remember what anyone else was doing. "I'm glad I'm here to hold her up," he commented. "Any suggestions for somewhere I can take her to get her mind off it? I think it would do her some good to get out and relax and just try to be alive for a few hours."

"Quiet Lake has a nice walking path all around it," Shulamit commented. "You can get directions from one of the guards outside. But be careful—if someone's done this to harass Esther, they may still be watching her."

"Don't worry, Majesty, she'll be safe with me." Eli beamed and even stood up a little straighter. "I'll look after her!"

Shulamit sent him away, and the guard outside the room shut the door once again. "Well, that's all of them."

"Lunchtime?" Rivka asked, stretching out her beefy arms. The lizard who was her husband ran down the length of one of them and hopped off her hand, transforming in midair so that he was human before landing on the ground. "Show-off."

"I must continue to impress you, Mighty One, as you impress me."

"Me? What did I do?"

"Stood there looking imposing, making sure our little queen can get through a morning of questioning witnesses without being challenged."

"Definitely a long morning," Shulamit agreed, standing up to stretch. "And we'll have to go over it all again between us. I just have to meet with those Imbrian traders about the cotton labor ethics thing first."

"Don't forget to take a ten minute break to clear your head," Rivka suggested.

"Fine, the first ten minutes of lunch, we talk about something else. Please tell the traders I'm ready for them."

♫

44

When Shulamit and Rivka got to the kitchen-house, Aviva was waiting with a platter of stuffed grape leaves. "This looks delicious!" Shulamit exclaimed and tore eagerly into her first bite.

Naomi played happily on the floor on the colorful cotton mat Aviva's father Benjamin had woven; cordoned in by a little wooden fence, she wasn't going anywhere and would be perfectly safe as long as the adults in the room kept an eye on her.

"How did it go in there?" Aviva asked.

"Lots of information that I need time to sort out," Shulamit told her. "Don't worry, you're about to hear plenty. I just need a few moments to take a break first."

"And then it'll all come erupting out from my brilliant volcano," said Aviva, a little starry-eyed. "I know how you work. I just wish I could watch you in there. I can't hide myself in your hair like Isaac can."

"Being a lizard has its..." Isaac paused, his hooded eyes narrowing and a sneaky smile oozing across his face. "...amusing side. Sometimes I hear the most interesting stories about Rivka, or, 'Captain Riv,' if you want to be accurate."

"*Nu?*" Rivka pushed an entire grape leaf roll into her mouth, and beneath the cloth mask they could see her face contorting wildly to chew it in one bite.

"They talk about your reputation."

"What of it? They don't doubt me, do they?"

"No, it's not that." He paused to drink. "The stories of valor in battle, I hear those all the time. Sometimes they get the details wrong—"

"I bet that frustrates you!" She grinned and he grimaced.

45

"It seems that a popular game in the taverns of Home City is to share outlandish superlatives about our own Mighty Riv."

"Outlandish superlatives?" Shulamit inquired.

"As one such legend goes, he wears the cloth mask not to protect his face from the hot Perachi sun, but to protect the sun from his face."

Aviva burst into giggles.

"There is another one that will make you laugh even harder," Isaac continued with a glint in his eye, "although I didn't like it. They say that Captain Riv is so tough that at only eight days old, he performed his own bris."

"Why, Isaac, whatever's wrong with that one?" said Aviva saucily.

"Ow," came the wizard's pointed reply.

Shulamit covered her face with both hands. "People must be really bored."

"I think they're creative!" Aviva was still grinning. "I want to play! Mmmm..." She bit her lower lip and stared into space dreamily.

"Apparently on Chanukah, Captain Riv doesn't need a shamash to light the other eight candles; they just burst into flame for fear of him," Isaac continued. "And on Passover, they say, 'If Captain Riv had been there, there would have been only one plague—himself.'"

"Terrific! Such confidence in me, they have," Rivka remarked.

"When he goes to temple on Yom Kippur to atone, the temple atones instead."

"What does that even *mean?*" Rivka held up her hands in exasperation, but she was smiling broadly enough that they could all see it even through the cloth mask.

"There's one that I have to remember to tell Riv later when you two aren't around." Isaac looked over at his wife slyly, and everybody watched her face grow red.

"I'll have to ask my regular farmers at the market if they know any." Aviva went back to the counter and retrieved a small dish of cooked mashed yam. After putting it on the table, she fetched Naomi from her makeshift playpen and sat down again with the baby on her lap.

"Hmm... how about, Captain Riv is so tough that he can't go near diamonds because he'll scratch them?" Shulamit took another grape leaf roll from the platter.

"I like it, but it only works if you know about diamonds being too hard for anything to scratch but another diamond," Isaac pointed out.

"Doesn't everybody know that?"

"Jewelers know that, but not everybody reads encyclopedias for fun," Rivka reminded her.

"Another one I heard," said Isaac, "is that 'his' temper is so fierce that, when he needs to shave, he just uses his sharp tongue."

"We should have a contest," Shulamit commented.

"No, we *shouldn't*," Rivka barked.

Shulamit giggled. "And point illustrated."

"Aww, Naomi wants to be just like Captain Riv." Aviva bounced the little girl, who grinned and flailed both arms at her family. "Look at her little mask!"

For indeed, the baby was now wearing the yam across the entirety of her lower face, just like the piece of cloth that hid Rivka's nose and mouth.

"About this case," Shulamit remarked. "As far as I can see it, there could be a number of motives for the theft—not just for money."

"I agree," said Isaac, nodding.

"I mean, resale of the violin is the obvious motive, but Liora's right—it wouldn't exactly be easy, now that everyone knows it's been taken."

"There are some people who still wouldn't care," Rivka pointed out, "if they really wanted something."

"They'd still have to be among the very wealthy," said Shulamit.

"Like the marquis."

"You just want it to be him because he's annoying."

"I should live long enough to see him shut up," Rivka grumbled.

"Anyway," Shulamit continued, "I also thought of Liora maybe taking it, or getting someone else to take it, to knock Esther out of the running as her competition. She says they're not competing, but maybe she was just talking."

"What about that other violin she's trying to sell?" asked Isaac.

"I noticed that. What if she wants Esther to buy that expensive violin the marquis won for her that she doesn't like?"

"If Esther were a different kind of person, I'd wonder if she'd hidden it away somewhere for publicity," said Isaac.

"I don't think anyone can fake the amount of distress she seems to be in," said Shulamit. "But I'm open to anything."

"What's your next move?" asked Rivka.

"After we rest a little, I'd like to go back to the inn and look at the building some more in the daylight," answered the queen after taking another drink from her cup. "Then I'd like to go to market. I still have Zev and Gershom to worry about—those jewelers. I want to see what state their businesses are in—how much foot traffic, how often people are actually buying things. I also want to see Tzuriel ben Kofi's stall. I don't even know what I'm looking for, but if I see it, I'll know."

♫

After lunch, while Aviva was cleaning up the kitchen and Shulamit was in her bedroom nursing the baby and resting during a brief rain shower, Rivka pulled her husband aside privately. "What was the rumor you didn't want to tell me in front of other people?" she asked in their own language, the guttural tones of the north.

"When there are no children around, people start telling stories."

Rivka furrowed her brow. "And you mean...?" she asked deliberately.

"You seem to have impressed them with your courage," he said evasively. She could tell he was teasing her, drawing it out.

"Yes, but you already said—"

"They've imagined us together."

"What?" A low growl, as if *she* were the dragon, came from somewhere in the back of her throat.

Isaac said calmly, "The short version is that someone or other started the rumor that one proof of your supreme bravery is that apparently I take you into my mouth *while I'm a dragon*."

49

"That's basically true, because your tongue is longer—" It took Rivka's mind a minute to catch on. There was a pause. "Oh."

Isaac nodded.

"*Oh*," his wife repeated.

"Usually when this one comes up, every man in the room is wincing, picturing an imaginary pair of dragon jaws dangerously close to his sensitive areas. They're quite impressed with you, Mighty One!"

"I hate this story."

"Would you trust me with that, if it were true?"

"What?"

"If you had one, would you trust me not to bite it off?"

"Yes, but—*oy*, the things they come up with."

He smiled at her, his eyes half-closed and speaking volumes.

Chapter 7: Everyone's Got His Quirks

When the usual brief afternoon rain-gust had exhausted itself, Shulamit strapped her baby to her chest with swaths of cloth that matched her papaya-colored dress and set out for the inn. She went on foot—the idea of trying to ride on a dragon while holding her baby terrified her, especially since her father's death had involved a fall from an elephant's back. Rivka and Isaac accompanied her as usual.

The shower had been heavy, but the sun was hot; puddles were already fading away as they crossed the city. By the time they reached the inn, the heat had driven Shulamit to buy a coconut from a street vendor. She drank it as quickly as she could so it wouldn't be in the way, and then stepped inside.

"Welcome back, Your Majesty," said the innkeeper. He looked uneasy. "Have you arrested anybody yet?"

"I want to look over the layout of the building, now that it's daylight."

"Of course. Please, take your liberty."

Shulamit walked straight through the lounge in front and into the open-air courtyard in the center of the building. Beyond the coconut palms and other greenery growing inside the inner garden, she could see two doors on each side opening up into the four inside rooms of the inn. One belonged to the traveling rabbi; the one next to him was where the old woman was staying on her way to the spa. They had accounted for each other's alibis. Esther's room was on the other side, next to the innkeeper's own quarters.

Skipping all of these for now, Shulamit walked through the courtyard to the kitchen at the far end. She peered nervously inside to make sure the room wasn't covered in gusts of flour. Not only would it not do to get herself sick in the middle of an investigation, but she still hadn't determined whether or not Naomi had inherited her digestive problems.

"All clear, *Malkeleh*," said Rivka, who had obviously perceived her timidity.

"Majesty!" exclaimed the head cook of the inn when the party made their entrance. The other workers bowed from the neck but continued busily peeling potatoes and shucking cloves of garlic.

"Peace, everyone," said Shulamit, grinning and looking as usual as though she was grimacing. "I wanted to look at the kitchen to see if there's a way anyone could have gotten into the courtyard through here last night."

"Not really," said the head cook, shaking her head. "See that grate?" She pointed with one finger, the rest of her hand wrapped around a zucchini. There was a large window, low to the ground, at the back of the room—but it was covered by iron bars that left no opening bigger than a melon. "That's how we toss out our garbage."

"Why is it like that?" Shulamit scrutinized the iron bars, holding her breath because of the smell of the pile of kitchen refuse outside.

The head cook rolled her eyes. "The owner was concerned it was a security risk. Lot of good it did him, in the end."

"So there really is no way anyone could have gotten in this way?"

The head cook shook her head again.

"What about that street kid—Micah?"

"Even he can't fit through those bars. Good thing too—the owner doesn't like him," said the cook. "I tried to get him to let me hire him to wash dishes or run trash out to the burn pile, but he's just—you know—prejudiced or something. Expects anyone who's living on the street like that to be trouble."

"Someone can be trouble because they're *in* trouble themselves," Shulamit mumbled absently, looking around.

The head cook nodded sagely.

"When you said, 'run trash out,' you don't mean the owner makes you take crates of trash out the long way, do you?" asked the queen.

"Unfortunately, yes," said the head cook. "We do the best we can with the window, but when you're talking about the skeleton of an entire lamb, or even just old crates themselves, with nothing in them—what the potatoes came in, or these zucchini—yes. We carry them out the front, and arooooound the building... It's okay. It's mostly a good job. Everyone's got his quirks."

The queen and her guards said good-bye to the inn staff and headed next for the marketplace. Zev's jewelry stall was deep within the thicket of merchants, and Shulamit sensed both of her fierce northerners slip into a state of heightened awareness as they tightened their orbit around her. Not that anybody expected her or her baby to be attacked, but they were there to keep her safe, and it was habit.

Zev was negotiating with a stylish-looking woman when they reached his shop. He and his customer paused their conversation to bow to Shulamit as people usually did when she entered a shop, then resumed their discourse. The woman was holding a rope of large beads that looked as though they might be lapis, turning it this way and that to catch different angles of light. Zev's face was a poignant study in eagerness trying to disguise itself as patience.

"I just don't know," said the woman. "I actually already have a lapis necklace... my husband brought it back for me when he was traveling to sell his cheeses."

"But perhaps it's a different style," Zev pointed out.

"Yee-es, it is that," she admitted. "If only I had my blue dress on, I could see if it works with the neckline."

"Try the clasp," said Zev, picking up another necklace that was in front of him. With deft fingers he showed her how easy it was to manipulate. Once it was closed, he tugged on it. "Strong, but easy to open and close."

"Oh, just like the one at Gershom's! Yes, I've seen that."

Zev gritted his teeth and bit his lip, his salesman's smile looking obviously forced. Shulamit grimaced unintentionally, her heart going out to him.

"I'm sure I've seen a necklace just like that among the queen's adornments," piped up a deep voice near Shulamit. "Lovely piece of work. Don't you think it suits her?"

Shulamit pursed her lips, suppressing a giggle. Isaac knew full well that she preferred more delicate jewelry and hadn't a thing in her closet that was dark blue, her least favorite color to wear. She suspected he was merely having a private joke with himself.

It was working. The woman, holding the necklace to her own throat, stole a look at the queen as she reconsidered. "Oh, Majesty, you have one just like—? You think I should—?"

"I think it looks very nice on you," Shulamit reassured her, speaking truth where Isaac had certainly not.

"Well," said the woman, a mischievous look of satisfaction creeping onto her face as if she were taking an extra cookie, "I'll take it. Maybe this means I should buy another blue dress, with a lower neckline to make room for it!"

While she and Zev briefly discussed the price, Shulamit turned to Isaac and murmured in his native language, "Why?"

"If Gershom wronged him, I want to help make up for it."

"Do we know that?"

"No," Isaac replied, his eyes twinkling and the edges of his mouth turned up slightly in an impish smirk. So she was right; sometimes he just liked to see if he could influence people's actions. Isaac, for all she loved him, was definitely someone to be thankful to be within his inner circle.

"Thank you, Your Majesty," said Zev when the happy customer had departed. He clasped his hands. "I have more lapis, if you want to see!"

"No thanks! Isaac's going to have to wear it himself, if he likes it so much." With that, she finally released the grin she'd been holding back for the past few minutes. That made Rivka laugh too. "So, how's business?"

Zev sighed. "Honestly, I don't even care if they're buying his necklaces at this point. I just can't deal with everyone coming in here and mentioning him. That clasp—my wife—she really had a mind for mechanics."

"May her memory be blessed."

"Thank you, Majesty."

"But the customers are still coming?"

"Yes, business is all right. I suppose. I don't know." He ran his hands through his hair. "Majesty, you believe me, don't you? I mean—"

Two young women rushed into the shop, panting and nearly crashing into each other. "Zev!" one shouted breathlessly.

"Yes?"

"We need tiaras. Cheap ones."

"Both of us. Maybe just something with wire?"

"We're going to a party."

"She was supposed to pick them up this morning."

"I thought *she* was!"

Zev's face creased into the first genuine smile Shulamit had seen on his face that day. "Relax! I can help you both, and it won't take long."

"We've still got to get to the hair-braiding lady!"

"I'll get out of your way," said Shulamit, heading back toward the entrance of the stall.

"Oh! Oops! The queen!"

"Your Majesty!"

The girls bowed and looked at each other with embarrassed expressions.

"Peace!" Shulamit waved and led her guards out into the sunlight.

"He's still got a healthy stream of customers," Isaac observed.

"Right. I was going to say," said Shulamit, "if we'd been in there for ten minutes and seen nobody, I'd almost wonder if he'd cooked this whole thing up just to get a leg up on Gershom again."

Chapter 8: Inside and Outside the Music Shop

Rivka, ever vigilant as the queen's personal bodyguard, was the first to spot a familiar figure several stalls down from Zev's, on the other side of the path. "Queenling—" She gestured to her left. "Tzuriel's stall, the man with the instruments. Isn't that him over there?"

"Oh! Well, that's lucky."

Rivka followed her across the street toward the makeshift music shop with Isaac close behind.

Tzuriel had his back to the road talking to somebody, but between his girth and the noticeably foreign locks of his hair, he was unmistakable. "Bye!" he called out, waving, as the other man left the stall holding a toy drum. "Come back and let me know how she likes it! Or even bring her by and let me see!"

Rivka automatically scanned the area for weapons. There was a dizzying array of musical instruments, many of which she'd never seen before and couldn't identify, but while the clutter allowed for several spaces where a blade could be hidden, nothing jumped out at her as an immediate danger. Tzuriel himself wore no blade; he was a large man but seemed generally mild and unthreatening.

"Peace," said Shulamit.

Tzuriel turned at her voice, and bowed when he realized who it was. "Majesty! And little miss Highness."

Shulamit, whose arms were already around Naomi in her sling, hugged her tightly and kissed her forehead. "We'd just like to have a look at your stock."

"Of course!"

Tzuriel's expression was a friendly one, but Rivka could still tell that it was twisted with stress. She knew Shulamit would play it cool—if he was innocent, there was no reason to risk the reputation of a merchant so new to her city. Shulamit prided herself on being a welcoming and hospitable ruler.

"I love to shop, so it's always fun to see who's new in the marketplace." Shulamit shot a look at Rivka, hoping she'd understand. Rivka acknowledged her strategy with a subtle nod. They were pretending to shop, to help Tzuriel save face.

He looked incredibly grateful.

Shulamit, her face deceptively placid, began to pore over the stock.

"Thank you," Tzuriel murmured as the two northerners followed her lead.

Rivka went straight to a stack of cases in the back. She knew the missing violin had been in one with strangely painted designs, and several of these were vividly decorated. However, none of them had butterflies, and most of them were the wrong size to be violins, anyway. One of them opened to reveal a trumpet within, and she thought of her days as a wandering mercenary on the battlefield of foreign kings.

From the other side of the store, she heard her husband's deep voice. "What's this one?" When she looked, she saw him gesturing at something that looked like a round metal basin upside down. It was attached to a long wooden pole by a single piece of string.

"You can play bass notes with that," Tzuriel explained. "Here, I'll show you." He put his right foot up on the basin and held the top of the pole with his left. "This is how you change the pitch." His left hand moved up and down the pole, holding the string. With a vigorous pluck of his right hand, he sounded a loud, resonating twang. "You want to try?"

"No, thank you, that's fine." Isaac smiled faintly and moved on to another instrument.

Rivka knew he wouldn't have been able to pluck the string without magic, as twenty years ago in battle, his right hand had been sliced open from palm to forearm, and the haphazard healing and resulting scar had left him unable to close any of the fingers. She didn't know what he was feeling just then, but it suited her to blurt out, "He needs no instrument. His voice is superior."

"Oh yes?" Tzuriel smiled and turned to Isaac curiously. "I mean, I can tell from the way he sounds when he talks, but you can carry a tune too?"

Isaac shot Rivka a look of impish affection crossed with mock humility. She grinned back at him; even though her mask covered her lower face she knew he would see the twinkling of her eyes. Then he rattled off a few bars of a meaningless drinking song.

Stirred though she was, as usual, by the way his voice carved caverns from the earth, she was a royal guard first. She compartmentalized her arousal and concentrated on searching through the instruments.

At the end of the row of cases there were some round metal pans she couldn't identify. They were as tall as her hand and as long as her forearm in diameter. Inside was a circle of shallow dents. The first thing that popped into her mind was *shield*, but the metal seemed too delicate and far too reflective for the battlefield— unless that reflectivity was to be used to deliberately blind the enemy with sunlight.

Tzuriel noticed her studying the object. "It's a steel drum. They come from the Sugar Coast, like me. Let me show you." He picked up one of the pans and hooked a strap around the handles on either side, then placed the strap over his neck. From a pile of mallets near what Rivka had recognized as ordinary animal-hide drums, he selected two and played a scale all the way around the circle of dents.

59

The sound was overly sweet, but it was loud and ringing and that appealed to her. "That doesn't seem hard at all!" exclaimed Rivka. She reached out with eager hands. Tzuriel quickly jumped in to assist her, perhaps out of fear she'd damage something in her wake.

The weight of the metal pan felt comfortingly solid around her neck. With a mallet in each hand, she tried the divots. "I like this!"

"Try to move your wrists rather than your whole arm," Tzuriel commented. "Like this. Fine-tuning. Also, try not to hit so hard."

"Riv? Hit less hard?" she heard Isaac quip to Shulamit across the room.

"I'm taking this with me," Rivka announced, fishing in a pouch for coins.

They finished searching the shop, but, thorough as they were, found no trace of the violin case painted with glittering butterflies. Shulamit, who had spoken with Esther personally and had a more specific idea of what the violin itself looked like, looked in all the violin cases they did find, but none of them suited her as their quarry.

Rivka found a way to use leather straps to tie her new steel drum to her back like a backpack, leaving her hands free as usual. Tucking the mallets into one trouser pocket, she followed Isaac and Shulamit back outside.

"Oh!" said Shulamit with surprise.

"Majesty," said Eli, whom she had found in the street.

Rivka looked him over. It was strange seeing him on his own; usually he was at Esther's side being solicitous and devoted.

"I was looking for Esther," said Eli, fitting neatly into Rivka's thoughts. "I thought she might be in the shop. Have you seen her?"

Shulamit shook her head. "We were just in there. She's not here."

Eli wrinkled his mouth. "She's really upset."

"I know," said the queen sincerely. "We're really trying. We're doing everything we can. We're just working methodically."

"I'm sorry. I didn't mean to—"

"No, it's fine."

"We were at Quiet Lake, walking, but she flared up at me. I was just trying to help her deal with what's going on. I was hoping she came back here so I could find her and talk to her."

"She's upset from yesterday; it's not your fault," Rivka reminded him. "She takes it out on you because you're close by."

"I just want to make sure she's okay." Eli ran his fingers through his hair. "She's needed so much comforting lately. I mean, she's usually pretty emotional anyway, and I hope I've been there enough for her—"

"I'm sure she knows how much you care about her," said Shulamit. "You barely leave her side."

"So you understand why I feel abandoned right now. Maybe a little unappreciated, especially since here I am, traveling with her in the middle of my studies." He looked around himself. "I hope she makes it back to the inn in time for Shabbat dinner. Sometimes I feel like she'd skip meals to practice if I didn't make sure she ate. I mean—What am I saying? She doesn't have anything to practice on right now."

Rivka tried to imagine being so caught up in practicing her swordsmanship that she skipped a meal but decided that the activity was too physical to permit such excesses. "She can maybe borrow one from Tzuriel ben Kofi in the meantime," she commented.

Eli glanced at the music shop. "That's why I thought she might be here."

Rivka, feeling an undercurrent of anger coming from him that she couldn't explain, found herself saying, "I just bought something from him myself." She jerked her thumb at the steel drum strapped to her back. "We have such a wonderful marketplace here, with so many things from across the world—but I'd never seen one of these until today!"

"Yes, it's a very nice market," Eli agreed, the mysterious negativity subsiding.

"You bought her a scarf here yesterday, right?" Shulamit asked.

Eli nodded. "Yes, somewhere on the southeast corner."

"That's where we're headed!" Shulamit looked at Rivka. "Maybe I'll stop in there if there's time after we talk to Gershom. Aviva's overdue for a surprise."

"Lead on, *Malkeleh*," said Rivka, eyeing the sky. They still had plenty of time to get back to the palace before sundown, and religion was far more relaxed here than it had been in her homeland, but it gave her a certain sense of devoutness and respect to *mark* the customs even if they weren't being strictly observed.

"Please take us there, Eli," said Shulamit. "Just so I don't embarrass myself poking around in the wrong shop looking for something that isn't there."

"And you'll get a chance to see the whole market, to look for Esther," added Rivka.

62

"Oh—yes! Uh, this way."

Rivka noticed him cast one final look at the music shop as they followed him down the street. It suddenly occurred to her that Tzuriel was an unmarried man, and that Eli might have realized the very same thing.

Chapter 9: Simple Gifts

Esther didn't realize how quietly she'd entered the music shop until she saw Tzuriel start. He gathered himself quickly and waved in greeting. "How long have you been there?"

"I just walked in." She bit her lower lip and looked away, her gaze sweeping over the rows of instruments. Looking at him felt complicated for some reason. Realizing her mouth had spread into an involuntary smile, she decided it must be from being around so many musical instruments. She wasn't sure what she was feeling anymore—was Eli right, that she was destroying herself with worry? That it would be healthier for her this way, to take some time off from performing? But—surely not. Not when stepping into a music store made her feel light-headed and a little bit like a Purim carnival inside.

Are you sure that's all it is? The smile renewed itself as she pictured Tzuriel, at a safe distance beside her, polishing a drum. Even though she wasn't looking at him, she was acutely aware of his presence. *Uh-oh.*

"Any news from the queen?"

She jerked her head back in his direction, reminding herself not to give in to silly thoughts, that she wasn't about to be disloyal to Eli just because he was... playing sour notes this particular afternoon. "No, nothing." Her smile had fallen away.

"You know, if you want—" He stepped closer and her breathing deepened. "—I have plenty of instruments. You can try out any one you like. Any one you think will work for you. Just tell me what you like in a violin, what characteristics you need, and I bet I'll be able to find something in my stock—at least for now."

"I—Thank you." Esther looked away. "I don't know if I can bear to think of shopping for a new one just yet." She adjusted the blue scarf around her neck as if it would somehow protect her from the way he was making her feel. "Wow, I didn't realize how many different kinds of instruments you had in here. From all over the world."

"That's what happens when you travel," Tzuriel replied genially. "Everything from my hometown's drums to flutes from places so cold they don't even take off their clothing to have babies."

She giggled at the unexpected image. "How do they keep their fingers from getting too stiff to play?"

"They have special gloves with no fingertips," he explained. "I have some in my stock, but I don't show them when I'm here in civilized countries." He rummaged around in a small trunk that she hadn't noticed earlier. "What do you think?"

"They're beautiful!" With wide eyes and a slightly opened mouth, she beheld the intricate embroidery of the fine textiles. "May I?" When he nodded, she felt the fabric between her fingers. "That's as soft as rabbits!"

"It comes from the musk ox," he told her.

"What's that?"

"It's a big hairy beast, like a cow—but fatter and hairier. And softer, and warmer." Then he chuckled. "Like me, maybe."

"This is so soft," Esther prattled.

Stop it, she said to herself. *Just because Eli said the way you were acting about your violin proved that you needed some distance from it doesn't mean you have the right to go embarrassing him like this. Look at how much he cares about you. He's traveling with you when he could be at home, getting ready for his law exams. He's worried about you.*

65

"Have you ever seen one of these before?" Tzuriel took the gloves from her with one hand, and in the other, he held up a gourd with some thin strips of metal stretched across its opening.

Esther shook her head. "What is it?"

"The two names I know for it are *mbira* and *kalimba*. Listen." Tzuriel put the gloves down and lifted his other hand to the little gourd. He cupped it in his hands and began to play the keys with his thumbs.

She watched him, captivated. What he played was innocent, yet haunting—rhythmic, yet soothing. It stilled the whirring of her tormented mind. Before long, she felt the stinging of tears in her eyes.

She didn't even realize she was reaching out for it until he stopped playing, mid-melody, and held it out to her. A welcoming smile on his face echoed his motions. "Try it." From anyone else, those words might have been a command, but here, it was consent. He was consenting to what she realized she was asking with her outstretched hand—and probably with her face too.

With her thumbs on the metal keys, she plucked a few notes. "Oh! They alternate," she realized out loud.

"Yes, to make it easier to play quickly."

More notes poured from her hands. She felt him close by and she was scared, but she held in her hands the source of her own strength, something with which she could create beautiful sounds. "It's so new and different."

"Sometimes people need a little different."

Eli thinks I need a lot of different, for my own good. She played faster, losing herself in sound, regrowing her missing wings.

"Esther, may I give this to you?"

66

"What?" She stopped playing and turned her face to his. Long rays from a setting sun slipped into the shop and hit her eyes just right, and she squinted and turned away.

"I know it can't replace your fiddle. But you deserve to be happy. And it's not that expensive anyway."

"I—" There were all kinds of reasons she should refuse. "Thank you!"

"It's a pleasure, really."

"Thank you," she repeated. "I'd... the sun is setting. I should get out of your way so you can pack up for Shabbat."

Tzuriel smiled and nodded. "Shabbat shalom."

"Thank you," she said again and left the shop with the curious feeling that she was escaping from something. But she held the kalimba to her chest, wrapped carefully in the new blue scarf.

♫

Shulamit dismissed Eli after he had shown her the shop that had sold him Esther's pretty blue scarf. As he headed off in the direction of the inn, she turned to her guards. "Maybe I'll have time to go in there after I talk to Gershom. The one in green looks like Aviva's style."

"We'd better get moving, then," said Rivka. "It's late."

"There's Gershom," said Isaac with a gesture.

Gershom was standing on the lip of his stall, chatting with a flamboyant woman who hovered just outside the lip of the stall next door. She was in the middle of a peal of raucous laughter when the royal party approached, accompanied by one of those affectionate swats of the hand that women sometimes do when a man has said something they want to pretend they've found outrageous.

"Oh! Your Majesty! So you've come to see my merchandise?"
Gershom was all smiles and deference.

The woman bowed slightly. "Majesty." Shulamit noticed that she
had a couple of jeweled barrettes in her hair that looked like
Gershom's handiwork.

"Do you know Dafna?" Gershom asked Shulamit.

"I think so. Your husband is the horse doctor, right?"

"Yes! That's me." Dafna stepped back slightly into her stall so
that she could spread out her hands at her merchandise. "I sell
scents. Scents and soap—massage oils, perfume—anything you
might need to smell nice."

"She started making it because her husband came home smelling
so badly from the horses," quipped Gershom.

Dafna grinned at him wickedly. "I need it, working next to you,
you big stinker!"

He smiled back at her, then returned his attention to the queen.
"So, what did you want to see?"

"I'm just here to observe," Shulamit said serenely and peered
around his shop. Business seemed to be healthy but not
overwhelming; a very old woman was peering carefully at a
display of earrings, and a pair of young people was looking at
rings together. She noticed a display of necklaces, but nobody
was looking at them. Maybe that meant something, but then, she
was only stopping by for a brief interlude.

"Majesty, here, I'd love for you to try something."

"What?" Shulamit turned and realized that Dafna had followed
her inside the jewelry shop. Instinctively she receded slightly
toward where Rivka and Isaac were standing.

68

"Here." Dafna dipped a glass wand inside a bottle and then held the wand up toward Shulamit's face—still, thankfully, at a respectful distance. "Smell this." From the look on her face she clearly felt confident it would be a winner.

Shulamit leaned forward and sniffed out of politeness, and had to conceal her surprise when she found she actually truly liked the scent. "That smells delicious! Like—baking. Is it cardamom?"

Dafna beamed, revealing a chipped tooth. "See? You know your stuff! You like it?"

"I do," Shulamit admitted. "What is it, perfume?"

"I have a perfume and a soap, and... I think I might have some of it left in the scented oil." She bustled back into her shop and began to rummage.

"Wait." Shulamit walked toward her with one hand up. "Do you have anything with ylang-ylang?"

"Of course! Everybody loves that. Old favorite."

"I'd like to smell the ylang-ylang massage oil." This way she could still buy something for Aviva without worrying about the scarf-seller packing up shop for sundown before she was ready to stop spying on Gershom.

"Decadent yet ladylike," Dafna commented, uncorking the bottle.

Shulamit grinned in spite of herself, thinking of how those words might very well apply to herself.

Rivka and Isaac drew nearer as Shulamit started counting out coins, and Dafna, who had been treating them as if they were part of the queen's clothing, suddenly registered their presence. "Gentlemen! Can I interest you in any scents? Maybe I have one that might enhance your... natural power!" She waved her hands around.

"I can pick up for my mother some more lavender soap," Rivka commented.

"Wonderful plan, Captain! Such a devoted son." Dafna fussed over her merchandise. "Now, let me see. Where did I...?"

While she searched, Shulamit scanned the names of the other scents. Litchi—one of her favorites. Rose. Jasmine. Clove. Magnolia. Pear. Raspberry.

Dafna saw her looking. "Which one do you have there?"

"Raspberry," said Shulamit.

"Ah!" said Dafna. "They don't grow down here. Too warm. I have to bring them in dried to make the scent. They grow straight out of the earth like little red jewels, each on top of a single flower that rises up out of the ground..." Here she mimed the actions of the imaginary flower, her hands spreading to represent blooming petals. "And at the center of the flower—one raspberry each!"

Shulamit, who knew better, shot a look at Rivka and Isaac. Rivka looked stony-faced; Isaac was smirking. They came from colder lands where raspberry brambles grew.

"Oops, there's the lavender. I'd stuck it in the wrong slot." Dafna grinned at them sheepishly.

"Thank you," said Rivka, handing over a coin and accepting the soap.

They drifted back into Gershom's shop. "She got you, didn't she?" He was grinning.

"The stuff sells itself," Dafna called over from the next stall.

"Did you want to look at anything in particular?" Gershom asked the queen.

"Yes. Hang on. I need my hands." She unwrapped the sling in which Naomi was riding and placed the infant crown princess delicately into Isaac's waiting arms. "I'd like to see a sample of your earrings, hair barrettes, shoe buckles, and one of those necklaces, of course."

"Certainly, Majesty."

Gershom turned to his stock, but she interrupted him. "No, wait. I'd like to choose them myself." He bowed in assent and withdrew backward to give her room.

She pored over the rows of earrings until she'd found the pair that looked as though it had the most sophisticated construction, then did the same with the barrettes and shoe buckles. Of the necklaces she wasn't so choosy, since she already knew about the clasp of questionable parentage.

"I'm just stepping into the light for a moment."

"Of course, Majesty, I trust you."

The outside light wasn't as helpful as it would have been earlier in the day, but it was better than inside the shop. She was able to get a good enough look, though, and carefully studied the design of each piece. The barrette seemed simple to open and close but was based on a completely different mechanism than the clasp of the necklace. The earrings were based on the screw principle and struck her as complicated and fiddly, rather than geared toward ease of use.

She walked back into the shop. "Thank you," she said to Gershom, dumping the pile of shiny objects into his waiting hands.

"Of course, Majesty. Will we see you again soon? I've just bought several tiny pale purple stones from across the mountains—I know that's your favorite."

71

"Mmm," she murmured absently. "I'm still researching you two."

"Oh, that!" Gershom shrugged dismissively. "He's just jealous. Haven't you ever had anyone be jealous of you before? Some woman, maybe?"

"Probably, but my world is more about women working together so we can all be better off. Speaking of which, it's time I got home for Shabbat. Aviva said she was working on a special surprise."

"Ooh, then don't be late! Shabbat shalom, Your Majesty! Captain, Sir." He bowed to the northerners as well as the royal party left the shop.

"*Nu?*" asked Isaac, bouncing Naomi slightly against his broad chest as they walked back to the palace.

"I could go either way, honestly," said Shulamit with some dismay. "The earrings show great skill and workmanship, but they're an absolute mess to open and close. The barrette was easy to open and close like the necklace, but it wasn't based on the same design. I keep changing my mind."

"He had plenty of customers," Rivka pointed out.

"But nobody was buying the necklaces," countered Isaac.

"Honestly? They're not as *pretty* as Zev's," said Shulamit.

"Isn't that subjective?" said Rivka.

"Probably, but it would explain why he stole the clasp design— to get a leg up on Zev's necklaces since his own weren't selling well enough on their own." Shulamit stretched. "If he stole it, I mean. And he's definitely been pushing them since the new clasp came out—that woman in Zev's stall had heard of it from Gershom first!"

"What do you think Aviva's surprise is going to be?" Rivka wondered out loud as the palace came into view before them.

"I *know* what it is, but she swore me to secrecy in case it doesn't work," Isaac piped up.

Shulamit grinned in anticipation and patted the ylang-ylang massage oil in her bag.

Chapter 10: Remember Shabbat and Keep It Holy

Aviva sat in her kitchen-house, trying to distract herself by reading romances. The surprise for Shulamit sat on the table before her, looming in golden splendor like a newly built palace in heaven, but it had no purpose until the time came for it to light up the queen's eyes. Driven by a zeal for bringing joy to her sweetheart, and for feeding and fueling that great brain of hers that ceaselessly worked like a team of little mice digging at the earth, she'd outdone herself. She'd had help, true, but then, that was what it was to be human—to need others, and to be needed by them in return.

Aviva loved being needed.

The story she was reading was very silly, but for someone who worked as hard as she did—especially now that they had a baby daughter to take care of—it was perfect in its shallowness. She wished she could find more stories about women loving each other, of course, but she'd had boyfriends before she met Shulamit and could appreciate a "rugged farmer" or a "handsome prince" well enough. Of course, none of the handsome princes ever seemed to do anything *for* their country, the way Shulamit was devoted to hers. Shulamit took her role as chief arbiter of justice in the realm of Perach very seriously, which was why she was out so late this afternoon.

Well, this afternoon Aviva had certainly been solving her own mystery, hadn't she!

With satisfaction, she cast her eyes for the fifteenth time over the golden mound rising from the table. She was just about to return to the story of the *Two Sisters Whose Boyfriends Were Soldiers* when she heard voices and footsteps outside. She closed the book. Her family was back, and it was time for the debut of her masterpiece!

♫

"We're back! Shabbat shalom! So what's the surprise?" Shulamit prattled as she pushed open the door. The first thing she saw was Aviva, sitting at the table, her hands folded over a book and her face full of love and pride. Then she saw what was in front of Aviva—

"Challah? In *here?*" For a moment her face furrowed with confusion and her eyelashes blinked rapidly. Then she realized. "Wait—"

"It's wheatless," said the goddess behind the table, standing and holding out her hands to flank it in gracious display. "I did it. Well, *we* did it, anyway." She turned her head to grin at Isaac.

Shulamit could do nothing but blink, stupefied. "It—you—it's really wheatless?"

"No wheat has entered this building in over four years," Aviva affirmed.

"But it actually looks fluffy! I thought you couldn't—you always said the dough got—" Shulamit was so excited that the ends of her sentences were getting swallowed up in frantic and meaningless hand movements.

"Oh, it did," was Aviva's calm answer. "For a while there, it was wet, lumpy sand, just like all those other times."

"But how did you braid it, without the wheat to make it pull?"

Aviva nodded to the wizard behind Shulamit. The queen turned to him, full of curious wonder.

"I used my magic to elongate its—spirit—I don't know." His expression was an odd mix of self-satisfaction and bewilderment. "I pulled on it with my hands in the air, without touching it, using magic to turn it into the way challah dough ought to be."

"This would have been a hard cake without his help," Aviva added. "And it's actually not really braided. I cut furrows into it with a knife and made sure to paint the egg into the cracks. When it baked, well, you see what it did."

"I can eat the challah with the others," Shulamit realized out loud.

"Exactly," said Aviva.

"I can be part of the blessing." Her face grew hot as blood rushed to her cheeks, and she felt sweet tears sting into her eyes. "Oh, Aviva!"

She pounced on her, throwing both arms around her neck and kissing her square on the mouth. Aviva smelled like baking. *Real* baking. "I can barely believe I'm not going to get sick," Shulamit murmured into the soft skin of her partner's neck.

"It should work," said Aviva. "There wasn't any wheat in here. Just a little bit of everything else, really—chickpeas, rice, sorghum... the yeast is from wine, of course."

Still clinging to Aviva, Shulamit turned to face Isaac, who was bouncing Naomi around and still smirking at his own contribution. "Thank you too, Isaac. Wow. I can barely believe it."

"I can," he chuckled. "It took us long enough!"

"Aviva, I've got something for you too." Shulamit fished around in her bag for the scented oil. "I found your favorite."

"Ooh, ylang-ylang! Aww, thank you!" Aviva sniffed at it happily, then set it on the table. "So are we all ready for dinner? Can I carry this to the main dining hall?"

"I think so. Are my braids—"

"YES," barked Rivka.

Aviva patted the thick black ropes of hair. "They're fine." She kissed Shulamit on the cheek and then picked up the challah.

♪

"Blessed are you, Milady, Queen of the World, who brings us bread from the earth." Shulamit had never before said this prayer with more triumph.

The introduction of a challah that Shulamit could actually eat caused quite the stir at the dinner table. Rivka's mother Mitzi, who like many people had never entirely believed the queen's claims of food-related sensitivities, asked the same questions over and over until everyone was relieved when Isaac just held up his hand and said, "Magic. It's magic."

"Oh, all right," she said vaguely. "It's not going to hurt me, is it?" She looked plaintively at Tivon, Rivka's second-in-command, who was also Mitzi's special gentleman friend.

"*Mammeh*, it's safe," Rivka reassured her. "Isaac would never hurt us."

The truth was that everybody knew Isaac would never hurt *Riv*, and that his umbrella of trust probably expanded to include the queen and her sweetheart and daughter, but outside that, nobody could really tell *what* he was thinking.

"So," said Aviva as she and everybody else tore into dinner, "where did the scented oil come from?"

"A woman called Dafna," replied Shulamit.

"Oh, Dafna?"

"We were at Gershom's looking at clasps, and her shop is right next door."

"I'm looking forward to trying it. I haven't washed in her rivers yet."

77

"Why not?" Shulamit's brow furrowed. Aviva knew much more about the market than she did. Had she made a mistake in her choice of gift? "Is it not well-made?"

"No, it's good quality... she just doesn't taste right." Aviva looked uncomfortable. "I don't want you to feel bad about your gift. As far as I'm concerned, it comes from *you*. But last week I saw her kick Micah in the head, just because she thought he was trying to steal soap."

Shulamit grimaced and shuddered. "She's not really the type of person I enjoyed being around. But I did want to pick up a present for you without having to go too far from the places I needed to visit on official business."

"I'm sure it's lovely oil," Aviva reassured her. "We can resanctify it later and take away any stink she's left in it with her attitude!"

Shulamit, who had some idea of what that might entail, felt warm inside, and also a flicker of arousal.

♫

Esther sat inside her rented room, playing on her new kalimba in the flickering light of the two candles she'd lit in observance of Shabbat. Her fingers barely brushed the flat metal keys; she didn't want anyone else to hear. For now, the kalimba, like her uncomfortable, suppressed thoughts about Tzuriel, were going to be her secret.

A knock at her door made her shake violently with surprise. The instrument nearly fell out of her lap, and she fumbled to catch it and place it safely on the bed beside her. For a moment, she didn't respond.

The knock renewed itself, and then she heard Eli's voice. "Esther, it's me. I figured you didn't want to miss Shabbat, and at any rate I've brought you some food."

Esther slipped the kalimba under her pillow and then slowly slid off the bed and walked to the door. "I have a headache."

"That's because you haven't eaten." He paused. "I've got lemon chicken with artichokes. The innkeeper was worried about you too, and he let me save you a plate. I worried about you all day. I'm sorry that I said things that upset you, before."

Lemon and artichokes. Truthfully, Esther *was* starving. The walk at the lake had been a hearty one, grown faster as they argued, and she had skipped dinner. And lemon and artichokes were among her favorite foods. "That does sound good," she found herself admitting.

"I'm sorry I upset you," Eli repeated.

She opened the door. "Thank you for bringing me dinner."

"Of course I'd bring you dinner! See, what would you do without me looking after you? I have to take care of you because you don't do it yourself." He looked a little bit disheveled. Had worrying over her done that to him? She felt guilty.

He hung around as she ate. "I looked for you before, but I couldn't find you."

"Where did you look? I was a little bit of everywhere."

"I thought you might have gone to Tzuriel's."

A little piece of artichoke went down her windpipe and she began to cough. He handed her water, and as she drank, she heard him asking, "Did you?"

"Yes, for a little bit."

"That man scares me. He's so friendly—too easy to like. Something's got to be wrong."

It was the perfect way of describing the way she was feeling. "You think?"

"I'm just looking out for you, Esther." He ran his hand down her arm. "I care so much about you. I feel so badly that I haven't kept you safe here the way I should have."

She still heard the words he had said earlier, at the lake, about wanting her to put down her instrument for a while. But here they were, these two who had known each other from their home village, alone in the big city that was full of thieves and wizards and suspicious, friendly foreigners. And she knew she needed him.

But she still didn't tell him about the kalimba.

♫

Riv Maror stole swiftly through the midnight-blackened streets. Others guarded the queen tonight; at Rivka's request, Shulamit had granted her permission to leave the palace and bring bits of Shabbat dinner to the youth Micah. She wished to draw nobody's attention and so she kept to the shadows, a bundle of food strapped to her back—inside the steel drum.

She had tracked Micah that morning and she could track him again, even if he'd found a different hiding place. For one thing, she had two years of experience as a bounty hunter—three, if you counted that first year guarding the bawdy house before she left her own land and became nomadic. For another, Home City had been her home for the past four years, so there was barely anywhere to hide a kitten, let alone a human teenager, without her having it on her mental list of alleys and attics.

Isaac wasn't riding along, even as a lizard on her shoulder. She wanted to respect Micah's need for privacy.

He had to be somewhere that he wouldn't be discovered and evicted.

He had to be somewhere without too much of an existing criminal element. They would have either turned him out or brought him under their wing by now—and he clearly wasn't under anybody's wing. Even the inn, who was feeding him from time to time, did so as one would feed a stray cat or dog, not as a protégée.

He probably moved around, but he probably had his regular places. And this was a kind of method to which she was well accustomed.

She found him at the fifth place she checked. Giving him the distance one gives a timid cat, she slipped into the alley but stayed where she was, not drawing any closer. "Micah, I brought dinner." Straight to the point, give him no reason to run.

"I'm not going back to the palace."

"I brought, well, it's *sort of* like challah, and there's lamb inside these pastries—"

"She thinks I'm a girl."

"I don't. And she won't," said Rivka gruffly. "But that's not important now. I've got food for you."

"That smells really good."

"That's the garlic." Rivka was smirking beneath her mask. Her own mouth watered as she remembered dinner, and she'd had a feeling he wouldn't be able to resist the smell. An unexpected sound came from the other end of the alley. "Is that a violin?"

"Yeah... I tried to play for money this morning, but Auntie Juice shooed me away."

"Maybe if we got you cleaned up people would be nicer to you and you could find a place to play without getting chased off."

"I'm not going back to the palace."

81

"I'm not trying to take you there. If I were, you'd know."

"Yeah?"

"I'm not the type to sit around trying to trick people. That's Isaac. I just grab."

He paused before speaking. "Yeah, I remember."

"See? I'm not grabbing now. Do you trust me?"

Another pause. "I guess so." There was a strange noise that Rivka figured was Micah setting the violin down carefully in the dirt, and then he came bounding up beside her. "What's the food in?"

"It's a drum from the Sugar Coast. I bought it from Tzuriel."

"You play?" Micah was starting to thaw, slightly.

"I guess I do now!"

"What's with this challah?" Micah asked through the gigantic mouthfuls he was wolfing.

Out of privacy for the queen, Rivka merely responded, "It was made without wheat as an experiment."

"It's not bad, just weird."

"Just different."

Then there was an awkward moment of silence before Micah finally responded, "Like us, huh?" He sounded bitter.

"I would assume you're made without wheat, like most humans," said Rivka.

"You know what I mean."

"Sure, although you pass better than the bread does," said Rivka. "You want to talk about it?"

"No," said Micah. "I mean—no."

"I'm not going to abandon you. I don't think I can," said Rivka. "Something won't let me."

The next noises told her, in the dark, that Micah was crying. They were tears of hot rage. "They act like I killed their daughter."

Rivka was a creature of instinct. "Your family?"

"I don't have a family."

"How can I help?"

There was more silence. "You wanna play?"

"Sure!"

The alley lay in between two workshops, so while they held back slightly, they didn't have to be as hushed as the hour might suggest. Micah scratched and scrawled on his fiddle, and Rivka tried to match his notes with the indented places on her steel drum.

"You know, in my country, some people don't even believe in playing instruments on *Shabbos*," Rivka commented after a while.

"That's stupid," said Micah, plucking a chord. "Don't they know that's where God goes to relax?"

Chapter 11: The Sabbath Bride

"He had a violin?" Ben stepped back, studying the hem of the dress Shulamit was trying on. Aviva was hopping around nearby doing stretching exercises, and in the corner sat Leah with Naomi in her lap.

"I know!" said Shulamit. "That's the first thing I thought when Riv was telling us about it over breakfast. But it can't—"

"Arms at your sides."

"Oh, whoops, sorry." Shulamit changed her position and tried not to fidget or gesticulate. It was unnatural for her, and of course her shoulder blades started to itch right when it was most inconvenient to move. "It can't be Esther's. I've been over it again and again and there's no way Micah could have gotten into the inn. I can't even blame magic, because if Micah had magic he wouldn't be living on the streets."

"Poor kid."

"Such a shame." Leah spoke in a hushed voice out of concern for the sleeping princess. "I gave him my last stuffed grape leaf the last time I saw him. I can't take everybody home, but sometimes I wish that I could."

"How's the length?" Ben held a piece of string to Shulamit's wrists, making sure the sleeves fell to the same level.

"It's good. I like how it cuts off a bit above my wrist, so I don't have to watch where I put my hands." Relief flooded her as she reached back, finally able to scratch her shoulder blades. "Micah... I wonder if his name used to be Michal."

"What's important now is that his name is Micah," said Aviva, both arms high in the air and her stomach stretched taut as if she were trying to touch the ceiling. "That's the boy who exists.

Anything else is a story." Her arms came down to rest at her sides. "Let him write his own story, just as you had to."

Shulamit digested these ideas as she continued to model the new outfit for her de facto father-in-law and official palace tailor. Micah confused her, but she wanted very badly not to fail him as his sovereign queen—especially since she had grown up with her own differences. For years, she'd been the only girl she knew who looked upon other women as romantic partners, and it had baffled her further that such feelings could happen in someone who felt no drive to emulate a boy in other ways. She'd made peace with her own version of normal many years ago, but Micah was her first intimate encounter with someone of his configuration.

"I'll try harder to understand. He's gotten the short end of the stick already, and I definitely don't want to make it worse."

"Speaking of violins," Ben piped up, "pretend like you're playing one for a moment. I want to make sure you have full range of movement."

The new dress was splendid, in a dark, bluish lavender, with sheer sleeves of paler lavender. The trousers he'd made were white to match the white embroidery across the dress, and so was the matching scarf. "This really is gorgeous," Shulamit couldn't help commenting. She lifted her arms and mimed playing a violin, making an awkward, self-conscious face because she knew she was probably doing it wrong.

"Everything is violins today," said Leah. "When we went to the public park this morning so we could eat a picnic breakfast on the lawn, Lady Liora was giving a surprise concert. Such wild and exciting music! That woman has a lot of energy."

"She said she was collecting donations so that Esther could replace her violin," said Ben as he rotated around Shulamit as if she were the center of a wheel and he its border.

"Mmmm," said Shulamit knowingly. "I bet plenty of people were saying that was just an excuse to get her name on everyone's ear."

"You know the public mind," Leah agreed.

"Would that matter?" asked Aviva. "Even if she was only doing it for attention, if someone's built a house, you can live in it even if they're strutting around on the sidewalk bragging."

"People talk like that whenever any woman wins notoriety," Shulamit groused. "They want us to be decorative and looking for attention, and then, if one of us is a little more blatant about going about it than the rest, she's blamed for being exactly the way they tell us we're supposed to be."

And for a brief moment, she was jealous of Riv.

"In any case, it was nice to listen to the music while we ate," said Ben.

"Feminism aside," Shulamit continued, countering her own outburst, "I do have to look at Liora's actions as potentially... convenient. She now has multiple motives for wanting Esther's instrument out of the way—not only does it silence Esther, but it gave her this excuse to—"

"It's Shabbat, Majesty the Workhorse!" Aviva wheedled, swinging her head from side to side. "You really should spend at least this morning relaxing. The whole reason God wants us to rest is so we'll be better to work once the rest is over."

Shulamit mock pouted and pointed to Ben. "He's working too..."

"Not really," said Ben. "I already did all the cutting and sewing. This is just fitting. I'm just... looking at it. See? She's all done!" He presented the queen to his daughter.

Aviva approached her. "She's gorgeous, of course."

Shulamit, who felt like she was nothing of the kind, but whose clothing was absolutely terrific, smiled awkwardly.

"And *now*, I relax. Now we all relax." Ben crossed his arms and nodded, satisfied with himself.

"I can make you relax," Aviva said in a very quiet voice, and Shulamit felt her blood stir. Naomi had been fussy the night before, and the bottle of ylang-ylang massage oil had yet to be opened.

"You can't say Ben doesn't know how to relax," said Leah through a smile. "Tonight he'll have half the guards in here playing Pirate's Payout and making themselves sick on cake."

"Only the off-duty ones, I hope!" Shulamit twirled around slowly, admiring the movement of her silky, diaphanous sleeves.

"I don't know," Ben joked. "In this room, I protect the priceless secrets of the queen's wardrobe! I might need some of the on-duty guards as well."

"You folks aren't gambling in here, right?"

Ben shook his head. "Only for imaginary points. We keep track of them and, you know, give each other a hard time about it if we get low."

Leah was shaking her head and rolling her eyes, but it was accompanied by an affectionate smile.

"I like that system," said Shulamit.

"It's perfect. We get to have fun and be as aggressive as we want, and there's never any danger of winding up in debt like that innkeeper of yours."

"My—inkeep—What?" Shulamit's ears perked up, and she became like a cat who's noticed a moth to chase.

87

"Oh, I thought you knew," said Ben chattily. "The man who owns that inn where Esther was staying. He's got terrible credit at the market. Even though the inn's always got business, he's got just as much debt. Some of us assumed it was from gambling, but, you know, we don't *really*—"

By now, Shulamit was practically vibrating. "That gives him... *so* much motive. And it doesn't matter if it's from gambling or opium or women—or men, for that matter—or something more boring like business speculation—I'll find out what it is and more importantly, if he—"

"Stoooooop." Aviva untied the ribbon that bound Shulamit's braids together and took a braid in each hand. "Relax. Just for a few hours. It's good for the brain."

"I guess," Shulamit couldn't help herself adding as she was pulled backward into Aviva's comfortably squishy chest, "people were watching the door and nobody saw the innkeeper go in there anyway."

"Naomi's comfortable here," said Leah, her eyes no doubt on their body language. "Why don't you two go off and get some rest while she sleeps?"

♫

"Now don't say the word *violin* until your clothes are back on." Aviva, whose arm held Shulamit around the waist, reached out with her other hand and moved Shulamit's palm forward to one of her generous breasts.

Shulamit, who had an admitted weak spot for such body parts, pressed against her greedily. "What's a violin?"

"You still said it! One point demerit in Pirate's Payout." Her face full of mischief, Aviva planted a lusty kiss on Shulamit's mouth. "Quick, to the bed, before our nest starts chirping again."

Shulamit lay back against the cushions and then noticed to her surprise that Aviva had uncapped the ylang-ylang oil and was working it warm with her hands. "But I bought it for you; it's your favorite scent and I wanted to pamper you..."

"Yes, it's *my* favorite," Aviva affirmed as she danced her slicked hands over Shulamit's feet and calves, kneading every tense muscle, "and here I am, smelling it up close. Makes perfect sense to me!"

"Mmm..."

"You know doing this makes me happy, and you also know you'll get your chance to make me boil over." The bits of Aviva's hair that came down around her face from her hairsticks brushed against Shulamit's leg, and she shivered happily.

"And then do I get my imaginary point back?"

"I was thinking of using it to season tonight's eggplants."

"Far be it from me to stand in the way of... *ohhhhhh*." Creeping fingers had spread up her thighs. "Oh, yes."

Shulamit's hips began to reach upward in a slow, rhythmic dance against the air. Even the sheets felt good beneath her hands as she clutched at them. She closed her eyes and truly, *truly* began to relax. When she finally felt Aviva's warm, wet mouth caressing her, she floated into a blessed delirium fed only by pleasure. Aviva was like a gentle but persistent sea, pulling on her in waves, and she was the grateful shore. And in her moment of ultimate vulnerability, she felt secure that that sea would surround her and rock with her and carry her home.

Aviva crawled up her body, leaving a trail of ylang-ylang oil and woman-love. When she lay on top of Shulamit, it was to be wrapped in womanhood, surrounded by the most exquisite, soft flesh. Shulamit kissed everything she could reach. Such intimate skin-to-skin contact made her climax continue well past the

89

departure of Aviva's tongue, like old raindrops falling from a tree after the storm has ended.

With a well-placed thigh, Aviva caught and nurtured the last few quakes. Shulamit felt wetness against her own thigh and deftly slid her fingers over. The two women moved together, with the queen's hand snugly between them, until Aviva, too, gave in to total abandon.

They lay together, each slightly tense knowing that Naomi's cries might be heard on the other side of the door at any minute, trying to soak up precious seconds of romance.

"Sorry; I got milk on you," Shulamit observed.

"It's been so fascinating to watch your body change..." Aviva traced the line of Shulamit's collarbone. "I watched you grow breasts. You taste like you did before you made a baby, though. That went back to the way it was."

"Trust my chef to be an expert in the flavor between my legs." Shulamit stuck out her tongue.

"There were some stupid boys at the market yesterday talking about women. They may have just been building boats from snow peas, but one of them said he thought women tasted like ripe figs."

"Figs?" Shulamit raised an eyebrow. "I don't think so. Are you sure he wasn't talking about the color, not the taste?"

"No, he definitely said taste."

"I would have said guava."

"I almost wish you'd been there to argue with him!" Aviva's eyes twinkled. "Imagine the look on his face."

"I just thought of a terrible contribution to the Captain Riv superlatives." Shulamit grinned wickedly. "But we can never use it, because nobody knows she's a woman."

"Uh-oh—"

"She's Riv Maror, right? For her horseradish personality? What if she tasted like—"

"Even if she were a boy, you could still technically make that jo—"

"Ew, ew!"

Naomi's fussing in the distance roused them from such frivolities. Shulamit clasped Aviva's body to hers with all four limbs. "I love you," she whispered. Then, the magic put away for next time, they both bustled about the room cleaning up with cloths and a basin of water.

"Don't kick over the oil!"

"You missed a spot."

"Where's my scarf?"

"Majesty!" called a voice from the hallway.

"Almost there!" Shulamit flung open the door and took her cranky infant into her arms. "Awww! Did you have a good nap?" She nuzzled her nose against Naomi's.

"I'll fix your braids while you nurse," said Aviva and followed her into the inner courtyard.

Chapter 12: Rat Who Wore a Dragon's Skin

The sweet, sensual aroma of oil filled Aviva's kitchen-house, marrying with the chopped garlic she'd set to frying in it. On the table was the dish of raw eggplant she'd sliced earlier, and she set the pan into the coals briefly so that she could retrieve it.

"Did you pick out this eggplant for tonight so you could match it to my new outfit?" Shulamit admired the brilliant lilac streaked with white.

"A complete accident," Aviva corrected her, "but I could buy violet vegetables any day and still stand a good chance to match what you're wearing." The eggplant slices went into the pan with a sizzle.

Naomi, sitting on Shulamit's lap, banged on the table and then made an ecstatic face at the noise she'd created. "Aaa!"

"Yes, little princess, you made a very good noise," said Shulamit, her nose buried in Naomi's hair. "Like Captain Riv with his metal drum."

Rivka, who was sitting on the other side of the table with Isaac waiting for their intimate family dinner, lifted an eyebrow. The corner of the mask rose and Shulamit could tell she was smirking.

"I want to run this by you," said the queen, changing gears. "What if our two cases are related?"

"What do you mean?" Rivka asked.

"Well, we've pretty much decided that if Gershom did steal the design, which I think we all think is what happened, then he must have used magic," said Shulamit. "Somebody *else's* magic, either for invisibility or shapeshifting or mind control."

Riv nodded.

Isaac opened his mouth as if to say something, but he must have changed his mind and waited patiently for Shulamit to finish.

"So, think about it. If someone connected to the Singing Hands case also bought one of the same potions or magic amulets or whatever," Shulamit continued, "then that would explain why the old ladies and the rabbi only saw Esther go into her room. And in that case, I don't think we're dealing with mind control, because all three of them plus everyone in the party would have had to be bewitched, and—can you even do anything that powerful with borrowed magic?"

"That's what I was going to say." Isaac beamed at his protégée. "If they *are* connected, then we're down to invisibility or shifting."

Shulamit grinned, feeling smart.

"Not that it matters between the two," Rivka grunted, "since selling either one is illegal." In Perach, magic was permitted, but certain kinds of magic that could easily be used for untoward pursuits were not allowed to be sold to those who had not spent years learning the magic themselves.

"And this is precisely why," said Shulamit. "The more I think about it, the more I'm convinced it was the same cheat. I mean— no one saw anybody but Esther go into that room. Barring the suggestion that she hid it herself to get publicity, which isn't likely given her level of genuine panic, no matter who else took it, it looks like a disguise is the only way it could have happened."

"Which means... what, that Gershom had something to do with this?" Rivka furrowed her brow.

"Not directly," said Shulamit. "But what if he bought the magic from the same place the violin thief did?"

"It would have to be a pretty big coincidence for two different people to be selling contraband magic all of a sudden at the same time," Isaac agreed.

"So if we solve one case, we solve the other," mused Rivka.

"If you can get the black market magic dealer to talk," Shulamit pointed out.

"If?" Rivka flashed her a confident look. "I don't 'if.'"

Isaac's mouth twitched impishly upward. His gaze of adoration had a hint of selfishness in it, as if he thoroughly enjoyed the way she made him feel.

"I *told* you that you'd think more clearly if you relaxed this morning," Aviva commented from the stove with a grin. "Now your river is bursting through the clumps of mud and twigs and flowing clear."

"We still don't know who it was," said Shulamit.

"List everyone again," Isaac suggested. "And their motives."

"Esther herself," Shulamit began, "for publicity. I don't think so. That grief was too real. And she's already Perach's sweetheart. Why do more?"

"I agree," said Rivka.

"Eli," said Shulamit. "Maybe out of some mistaken idea she needed his help with publicity? I don't know. It's not very likely. Liora. She never left the table, but the marquis did, and they come as a matched set."

"And her motives are obvious—she got to look like a saving angel this morning at the park, and plus, Esther's her competition," said Rivka. "And that other violin she's trying to sell."

94

"I don't know how seriously to take all that competition chatter," said Shulamit. "I don't like it that just because they're both the two most famous women musicians in Perach, they automatically have to be competing with each other. People never want to see women as supporting each other. It's always got to be this narrative about who's prettier or who's more beloved or whatever. Ugh."

"But you can't ignore it as a motive," Rivka pointed out.

"You're right. Sadly, I cannot." Shulamit looked around the room grumpily, musing. "But just for the sake of my nerves, I'm going to concentrate on her extra violin. So maybe it *was* the marquis."

"He could certainly afford black market magic," agreed Isaac.

"Maybe we should look into Liora's jewelry and see if any of it was made by Gershom," said Shulamit. "That would be a connection between them. Say Gershom was making her a new set and they happened to start talking..."

"We can do that in the morning," said Isaac.

"Then there's the innkeeper," Shulamit continued. "He's got no credit at the market."

"He does pay his workers on time," Rivka pointed out.

"Your point?"

"That he's not a complete *chazzer*."

"He doesn't have to be to steal from his guests, especially if he thought they were well-off and could afford it," said Shulamit. "Maybe he stole it so that he could *keep* paying his workers."

"If he has no credit at the market, how could he buy the magical device?" Isaac mused.

"Maybe he promised the seller a share of the—"

"But that would be *credit*."

"Hm." Shulamit looked at the corner of the room.

"AAaaa!" Naomi banged on the table again.

"We're ruling out Micah because he couldn't pay for magic, either, right?" asked Rivka.

Shulamit nodded. "Plus, he'd use magic to find food or... make his voice deeper or something, wouldn't he? If he had it?"

Rivka nodded slowly, as if she was thinking about it.

"Lastly, there's Tzuriel ben Kofi."

"Who sells instruments," said Rivka. "Who travels."

"I know," said Shulamit. "And he's at the market all day too, where Gershom is. Maybe the person selling the magic migrates from booth to booth until he or she finds someone who seems susceptible and likely to buy."

"So we're down to—the marquis, Tzuriel, or the innkeeper," said Rivka.

"And I'm down to this eggplant," said Shulamit with a grin as Aviva returned to the table carrying a pan brimming with savory-smelling delights.

♫

A full moon lit the queen's private garden, well enough that she could see the path in front of her to walk safely. She paced through the rows of trellises with their winding vines of passionflower, showy and outrageous, and paused to inhale the decadence of the jasmine. She was pleased with herself for how far she'd come with her mysteries, the solving of which she regarded as one of her favorite royal duties.

Aviva and Naomi were off spending quality time together, and she'd finished reading last week's collected agricultural news from across the kingdom, so it was a perfect opportunity to do some hard-core thinking. She did realize that the magic theory meant that an outsider could have gotten in and taken the violin, but it would still have to be fenced, and an outsider wouldn't have known which room was Esther's in the first place. She admitted to herself that the idea of the marquis being a contemptible criminal appealed to her, because he'd hurt both her pride and her sense of feminism by his crass comments. But equally did the idea of *Liora* being guilty of anything repulse her. She'd heard the two-faced nature of the public's comments about her—that she was talented and sexually enticing, but also that she was addicted to the attention, and the way they assigned to her all sorts of jealousies and fits that may or may not have been justified.

Well, maybe the marquis had done it on Liora's behalf without consulting her. Shulamit liked that idea.

But Aba didn't leave you the throne to "like" versions of the truth, she counseled herself. In her heart she hugged the image of her father and resolved to pursue justice.

She heard movement, and noticed that Isaac was also walking in the garden. "I feel good, but I'm not there yet," she murmured quietly. The garden was the kind of place that invited quiet, especially at night.

Isaac simply smiled at her.

Shulamit felt something that could have been an insect brush against her bosom. When she heard a soft noise on the ground, she realized that she must have dropped something. Two fingers to her ear confirmed the event. "My braids must have pulled it off."

"I'll get it," said Isaac, bending down.

"I'll have to have the hook adjusted," Shulamit continued. "They always do that if I don't—" Then her heart began to pound heavily, and blood rushed into her face.

Isaac was picking it up with his right hand.

His disabled, scarred right hand. *The hand that couldn't close.*

Aba Aba Aba, ran her internal monologue, screaming out in prayer. Then she felt the voice of God stilling her, descending around her like a royal mantle. So. They'd just been talking about shifting potions. Maybe she was right. Maybe this wasn't Isaac.

She had to test him. She had to make sure.

"Thank you," she said, in as friendly a voice as she could manage, desperately hoping she didn't sound as panicked as she felt. Or was it excited? Because—because if she could *trap* this man—be he the marquis, Gershom, or anybody else—she could find out who was selling it. She wished she had some way of calling for Rivka, but if it was truly an impostor, that would almost certainly scare him off.

She had to know.

To buy time, she squeaked out the first thing she could think of. "Do you think these earrings suit my new clothes?"

"They do, Majesty." He spoke with Isaac's voice, even Isaac's accent.

Well, she couldn't just *demand* that he speak in Isaac's language, not without rousing his suspicions. And that would still prove nothing, because it was the native tongue of thousands of people besides Rivka and Isaac anyway.

Rivka.

An impostor wouldn't know about Rivka being a woman.

"I've been thinking about those stories they tell of Captain Riv." She tried to make her voice light and airy, to sound amused. "You know, all the ridiculous ones we were laughing at earlier."

"They are terrific, aren't they?" the maybe-Isaac agreed.

"I think the most ridiculous is the one where they say he performed his own bris even though he was only eight days old," Shulamit continued. She was fiddling with the ends of her scarf like mad, and the sweat on her palms was doing unpleasant things to the fabric. "What do you think of that?"

"Oh, well, you know Riv," said the man with a chuckle. "It could have happened just as they say. After all, I don't know—I wasn't there!"

I've got you, thought Shulamit, and a wave of energy suffused her body. *And now I will trap you like the rat you are.*

Fear flashed into her mind for a moment as she considered the possibility that the impostor might be there to inflict violence or even molestation on her person. But they were alone together in the garden, and he seemed all too willing to keep his distance, now that he'd handed over her earring. Nothing about his body language felt threatening, and in fact, she should have known he wasn't Isaac all along. Even though he towered to Isaac's height, and even though his torso was as broad, he seemed somehow more of a lump than a great majestic cedar tree. He had Isaac's form, but he didn't have the power of soul to command it as Isaac did.

No, he was here for some other reason. And the large, empty-looking bag he was carrying by a shoulder strap gave her a pretty good idea why. "In any case, I'm glad Riv has such a fearsome reputation. It's good for the palace." *Continue the meaningless small talk. Keep him here while you think.*

Shulamit had to lure him somewhere there would be enough guards to overpower him quickly, but also somewhere he would

99

find the bait plausible. She first thought of the treasury but couldn't think of a reason to suggest visiting the royal vaults late at night.

"Yes, Riv is quite an amazing man."

Don't laugh don't laugh don't laugh. "I suppose you feel pretty lucky too." Then she almost kicked herself. What if the comment scared him away somehow? She didn't want him to feel pressured to perform for her, to come up with new remarks. She had to keep him by her side until she'd figured out a way to trap him. "I'll tell you something else I feel lucky about. Him bringing his mother to the palace. One more set of hands to watch the baby. She's such a nice person. And it doesn't take very much to keep her happy— I'm grateful for that." Prattle, prattle. "Just clothing and jewels, really—"

Jewels. *Yesssss.*

She studied his face as surreptitiously as she could. Did she detect a note of excitement at those last words of hers? Jewels. So she needed to lure him with the promise of her jewels. But they were in her private dressing room, which adjoined her sleeping chamber, and there were definitely no guards in there.

"Some women are easy to please," the impostor agreed.

"I am, too, in a way," Shulamit found herself commenting. "Just give me a good book and something violet to wear." Wear! Her clothing—her clothing came from Ben, and in Ben's room *right now* all the off-duty guards were playing their game.

If she could only—

"Anyone can see your love for the color violet," said the impostor, "on your lovely new clothes."

"That reminds me, Isaac," she said carefully, laying a trap with every word. "I'd love your opinion on my new necklaces. After all, I love jewelry too."

100

"Oh?" He definitely seemed interested. She'd seen that look before, on the real Isaac's face—but about Rivka, not jewels.

"I don't know which to wear with my new outfit," said Shulamit. "One is—" She thought frantically, trying to figure out what would be ridiculously easy to fence. "—dozens of tiny diamonds, strung on chains so delicate they seem nearly invisible."

"Sounds very lovely, Majesty." The look on the impostor's face reminded her of a dog anticipating table scraps.

"And the other—well, as you know, I'm tiny, so I don't like to wear something so large as the gold one," said Shulamit, knowing that gold could be melted down for resale. "But I'm tempted by its amethyst stones. There's my love for violet again."

"They both sound like they'd suit your new clothes," said the impostor. "Perhaps I could—"

"Would you look at them for me and give me your honest opinion?" Shulamit could barely breathe, but she forced herself to smile. "Without my father here..." She looked away at the passion blossoms dramatically and sighed, feeling secure in some way of the heart that he *was* there, in that moment, guiding her. Princess Brainy, he had called her.

"Of course!"

"I've left them in the dressmaker's studio. I meant to try them on earlier when we were doing the fitting, but then the baby—"

"Yes, I understand."

"Can you come with me now? It should be quiet in there."

"Lead the way!"

To your downfall, you rat. She did her best to walk casually out of the garden. If she moved too quickly he might get suspicious. But she was also afraid he'd lose his nerve if she went too slowly.

101

They passed a couple of servants scurrying around, who bowed to the queen, but she didn't give any sign to them that the man beside her wasn't Isaac.

With every passing moment, she grew more fearful that he'd know something was wrong. She couldn't lose him now. Better tempt him further. "Do you mind if I leave you alone in there for a few moments while you look at the necklaces?" she asked the impostor. "I want to go check on Naomi. All the leftover scraps of fabric from the tunic and the trousers are still piled up on the worktable, so you can just hold the necklaces next to them and let me know what works."

"Oh, that's fine, Majesty!"

She could tell now that he, too, was doing his best to hide his emotions from leaching out into his voice—in his case, unexpected rapture. *Majesty, not "Malkeleh,"* she couldn't help noticing. *Well, I guess we're all lucky he isn't very good at this.*

"Let me just slip in there for a moment to make sure Leah isn't undressed," Shulamit murmured. "I could never forgive myself if I interrupted her privacy like that."

"Naturally, Majesty."

When Shulamit touched the door handle it felt rough and clammy in her nervous hands. She opened it a sliver and slid inside quickly, shutting the door behind her. "Everyone!" she hissed.

In the golden lamplight, she saw that half a dozen guards were seated around a low table on the floor. They'd been silently studying Ben, who was deciding his next move in Pirate's Payout. At her entrance, all eyes moved toward the door.

"The man with me isn't Isaac; he's an impostor. Capture him instantly and ask no questions 'til he's yours." She barked out these orders in a *sotto voce* hiss, but clearly enunciated.

"What?" one of the guards asked, but they all readied themselves.

Shulamit opened the door slightly and stuck her head out. "All clear, Isaac! Leah's not even in here."

The door swung open, and Shulamit stood back to avoid the commotion as the guards seized the pretender. "What? What are you doing?" he demanded to know. "I am Isaac! I am your commander's favorite!"

Shulamit ignored his appeals and simply stood back and watched. When he had been secured and forced onto the ground, glaring at everyone, she simply muttered, "Good work."

"What's going on?" asked Ben, who was still holding the game piece with a look of confusion on his face.

"This man has gained admittance into the palace by using some form of magic to pretend to be Isaac," Shulamit explained. Shouting and clamor erupted from the guards.

Then, from the shadows in the corner of the room, a shape emerged. It was Rivka, wearing her steel drum by its shoulder straps. She bounded across the room in only a few strides, the visible parts of her face red and her eyes explosively angry. Shulamit had never seen her so furious before. She watched, silently, as Rivka marched straight up to the prisoner.

Crash went the drum over his head, and he slumped over. Rivka's shoulders moved like the curls of a whitewater rapid and she was breathing heavily.

"Wait, no, Riv—we need to question him," Shulamit found herself saying.

"He's not dead," barked the captain. "Just knocked out."

"Good."

"Captain!" protested one of the guards, who were all looking at Rivka in horror. "How could you do that without knowing for sure it wasn't really Isaac?"

Rivka simply cast them a look of scorn as a familiar lizard crept out from within her voluminous barbarian hair and crawled to the top of her head.

"Look, he's changing!" Ben pointed at the intruder.

"His control on the magic is slipping because he's unconscious," explained a deep bass voice coming from the lizard on Rivka's head.

The guards hastened to tighten the ropes around the prisoner as he shrank into the size of an ordinary man. His skin darkened; his hair grew longer. "Wait, I know this boy," said one of the guards.

"I do too," said Shulamit grimly. "He was at the booth with the juice seller the day of the violin concert."

"Yes, I think he's her nephew," said the guard.

"He's starting to wake up," said another guard.

Shulamit walked up to Caleb and crossed her arms in front of him. He groaned, so she hoped he could hear her.

"You idiot," she growled. "I have a *baby*. I haven't worn real jewelry in six months."

Chapter 13: The Thorny Rose

Rivka paced outside the security cell, a wolf on the hunt. Inside, Caleb was alive, but he swung in and out of consciousness like a broken door. The palace doctor was insisting that he be allowed to rest until morning, so a few of the guards secured him before leaving him be. When the last of them left, she tried to enter.

"Riv, no."

She turned, looking at the queen. "What?"

"You can't go in," said Shulamit, small but commanding, as Rivka herself had taught her. "You'll kill him."

Rivka paused. "No, I won't." Even as she said it she knew she was just saying words. Would she? How could she not?

"Right. Riv, that was scary, but we need him alive. We need to get him to talk."

"What he could have done—" Her hands balled into fists so hard, she felt her nails digging into her skin and almost relished the pain because it felt like combat.

"He was only here to steal." Shulamit's voice was quiet and calm. "But whoever sold him that magic could sell it to someone else, and next time, they might not just steal violins or copy trade secrets. We could have a murderer on our hands unless we put a stop to this, and he's our best clue."

Rivka's skin crawled, and she wanted to hit something. The stench of a violation she could not put words to hung all about her in the air. "I... am... *so angry*."

She shivered as Isaac's tiny lizard feet scampered down her body so he could reappear in human form just behind her. When he was there, she leaned back into him gratefully, feeling the stone masonry of his bulk support her weight.

"Your anger is justified, every bit of it," Isaac reassured her. "Now, if you could redirect it for now, and save it up until tomorrow morning, you'll be able to use it to our advantage."

"You hear that?" Aviva, who had come floating in with the infant princess asleep in a wrap after the commotion was over, commented to Shulamit within earshot. "Fletching. He doesn't take away Rivka's arrows; he just helps her aim."

"Isaac, go wear her out," Shulamit commanded. "Go... spar, or something." She spoke confidently, but she was hovering awfully close to Aviva and the baby.

Rivka eyed her critically. "Are you sure?"

"Tivon's got everything under control. Go rest. I need you to intimidate him in the morning, not be falling asleep because you stayed up all night stomping around."

"Yes, Queenling." Shulamit was right. And what she needed— "Not sparring," she added, just for Isaac, in their own language. The look she gave him wasn't flirtatious—it was a pleading demand.

They went back to their room without another word.

He closed the door and began kissing her, thoroughly, nurturingly—but with the force that she needed. She pushed against him, craving contact in every way. Her fingers took comfort in the bulk of his chest, his arms, his back. This was real. This was Isaac.

"You're safe," she found herself saying. *Oh, so that was what this was about.*

"How could I be otherwise?" he purred in his deep voice, touching her in ways that made her feel as if she had the sun itself between her legs. "My Mighty One defends me."

They made love quickly, his powerful thrusts giving her energy something to complement besides rage and offense.

"You don't have to worry about anyone attempting *that* nonsense again," said Isaac. "Some of those guards are tremendous gossips, and by afternoon, stories of your reaction will be all over the marketplace. Who would want the legendary Captain Riv after his throat, held back only by the queen herself? In the morning, you'll take that anger, and when you direct it at that foolish young man, he'll fear you and he'll give us exactly what we want."

"Mmmhmm..." Rivka was gazing at Isaac's face up close, finding solace in the familiar features.

"And I'll watch you do it and fall in love again."

"Your arms feel good around me. Hold me everywhere." She wanted to feel his body like a heavy blanket; she wanted him to be the realest thing, and the closest.

"Every time I tell you I love you," he murmured as he wrapped her in his cloth-covered muscles, "I know how lucky I am to be able to tell you at all."

She rested her head against his biceps and listened; she knew the story he was leading into, and she found its predictability comforting—especially when flavored by the vibrations his voice caused in her body at this close range.

"When I was under the curse, so many years ago..."

It had only been four years since she and Shulamit had lifted the curse that had imprisoned his human form in a mare's body—a mare that could still turn into a dragon but had lost the power of speech—but in that time, they had grown so many wonderful relationships that in some ways it seemed remote. Still, it was easy to put herself back there if she thought about it—her, roaming the lands as a lone mercenary, and he, the horse she rode without realizing it was the man she'd loved, whom she believed dead in battle.

"...Every moment of those three years I loved you. I loved you when I was a dragon, the only place my human soul still lingered; I loved you when I was a horse and could only think of you as 'my shiny.'"

She caressed him, listening peacefully.

"I loved you, and I badly wanted to tell you," Isaac continued. "But the curse took away my voice, and left me illiterate as well. So I had nothing left but my loyalty."

"But you knew I still loved you because I called to you when I touched myself." Now that she knew that the dragon she'd slept against had been him and not just a beast, a pet, a steed—she wished she'd said more at the time.

"I did, and I told myself that such privileges should have been enough—sleeping curled up around you, knowing you still cared."

She snuggled into him. "What kinds of things did I moan?"

"Just my name. Sometimes I wondered what you'd do if I shifted my tail to help you along."

"If I'd only known it was you..."

"But you didn't, so the most loyal thing I could do was restrain myself. To do otherwise would have been betrayal. If I had, you might have killed me or at least left me to myself, and you'd have been right."

"I know *now*," she barked, moving his hand between her legs.

He smirked with admiration as he grasped at her with practiced fingers. "Insatiable woman!"

"Greedy dragon," she retorted.

"Mighty One."

Slowly his fingers moved in and out of her and she grew languid in his arms, still listening to the story. Not every act needed a direction. Sometimes, things just felt good.

"Then, one day, I remembered that there was still one dignity of a man's life that I could still manage. I could bring you flowers."

"Roses."

"I could bring you roses. I tried to clasp a rose from the rosebush, with my left paw..." He curled the fingers of his left hand inside her, mimicking the action, and she threw her head back in pleasure. "...My claws could easily separate it from the bush, but it fell to the ground. I tried to pick it up, but the stem was so tiny and my claws were so big that I couldn't curl my fingers tightly enough to grip it. I kept trying, but they were all the same. And when I tried to bite it off, I got a mouthful of thorns."

"Your poor mouth." Rivka ran her fingertips over his lips, and he responded by nibbling them.

"I knew I couldn't think too hard about it, or I'd slip back into that awful horse form."

"Shiny!"

"Yes, you were my 'shiny' when I was a horse." He still sounded a little embarrassed about it. "I didn't know what was male and female; I just knew that whatever the stallions wanted from me in my mare form, I very much didn't, but I wanted it with you, and that you were my shiny."

"Sorry for those times."

"Forgiven." He kissed her on the nose. "Finally, I just grabbed the whole rosebush out of the ground in my back paws, and I flew to the bank of the river where you were bathing."

"You liked it when you saw me bathe."

"I *still* like it when I see you bathe. So, you stepped out of the river, your hair wet and dripping down your body..." He painted his right hand down her body, following the water's path. "Your muscles were toned and shining with water, and I struggled to stay in my dragon form."

"I just thought I was naked by myself, taking a bath. I remember you bringing me that whole rosebush and thinking to myself how little I understood about dragons."

"I laid it at your feet."

"I picked one single rose and smelled it."

"And you patted me on the head. For one moment I was a man again—a real man."

"I asked you—"

"You smiled at me, and you said, 'You strange beast! Couldn't make up your mind which rose, so you had to take them all?'"

They said these last words together. This was not a new story.

"No," Isaac intoned. "I knew which rose. My rose... my rose is thick and sturdy enough that she would fill my grasp rather than slip through my fingers. My rose..."

They kissed.

"But then you turned back into a horse."

"I couldn't help it. You were standing over me so powerful, so perfect."

"And you started to eat the rosebush."

Isaac chuckled. "Indeed."

Rivka grinned back, understanding his double meaning.

"Harder..."

Chapter 14: Good Cop

The doctor told Rivka and Isaac that when Caleb had woken up in the middle of the night to urinate, he was medically out of the woods and fit to question. Since the two of them were still asleep themselves, Caleb's guards simply tied him back up and waited until morning, and let the delinquent return to sleep.

Now it was morning, a bright, clear one, and the pair entered Caleb's cell. They stood against the wall, watching him sleep. Rivka was powerful and in control; anger still flowed through her, but it served her rather than controlling her. She also felt happy and sexually satiated.

"You were perfect last night," she said to Isaac in their native language, since there was nothing to do until Caleb woke up. The two of them had discussed it and thought it would be psychologically intimidating for him to wake up to their presence naturally.

"Of course I was," said Isaac smugly. "It's what you deserve."

"You were everything I needed you to be."

"Shapeshifter!" He smiled wickedly.

"You know that's not what I mean." Then Rivka remembered some details. "Well, maybe a little bit."

"I *thought* you liked that."

"I like everything. I like *you*."

A noise nobody but two trained warriors would have heard came from the far side of the room. Caleb had swallowed. Rivka heard the clenching of his jaw and could tell he was awake. She met Isaac's eyes with her own and then turned back toward the prisoner.

112

"Wake up, you dog. That is your name, isn't it? Caleb?" Her words were a percussive sneer.

Caleb just groaned.

Rivka stalked to the bedside in a single step and towered over him. "You're new in Home City. I don't like it when people bring trouble to my town. Have you heard of me?"

"Mmmhmm," Caleb whimpered.

"What?" Rivka kicked the bed.

"Yes, sir."

"Who am I?"

"You're Captain Riv... sir."

"And what's my job?"

"You—guard..."

"I protect the queen." Rivka gripped the bed with both hands and jostled it up violently, tipping Caleb toward the wall. "Do you hear? I. Protect. The. Queen. You really thought to mess with me was a good idea?"

"I wasn't going to—"

"I don't care! And who says I believe you, anyway?" She jerked the bed again, and only Caleb's restraints kept him from being smashed into the wall on the other side of the bed.

She knew they were protecting him, of course.

"It was only a joke."

"*Am I laughing?*" shouted Riv.

"No—"

"Do I look like I'm laughing? Isaac, he thinks he's a comedian. I don't see anything funny here. Where did you get those powers?"

Caleb said nothing. Rivka's warrior instincts told her he'd suddenly thought of someone else to fear—the name he was protecting.

"My turn," Isaac murmured in their native tongue.

As Rivka withdrew, she watched Isaac approach the bed with warmth on his face. Maybe he could win the *schmendrick*'s trust and convince him to confess his supplier that way.

"I'm Isaac," said the wizard to the prisoner. "You seem like you'd be a fine young man if you weren't trying to steal from us."

Caleb's eyes widened and he strained against his bonds. He didn't say anything.

"Now, you've met Riv—you've heard of Riv, and you know what he can do. I don't think you want that. I think you'd rather talk to me, because I'm not as angry as he is. I can be nice to you. All we need to know is the name of the one who sold you the magic you used last night."

"I don't remember," Caleb murmured nervously. Naomi would have been able to tell he was lying. Rivka eyed him critically; he was almost vibrating with fear.

"Maybe we can protect you from whoever you're scared of. If, you know, you can help us." Isaac sat down on the edge of the bed and Caleb yelped.

"Dafna! Dafna with the soap. *Don't touch me.*"

♬

"That was quick," said Shulamit, who was waiting for them in the courtyard just outside the detention area. Someone had brought her a chair, and she was nursing Naomi under a dragon

114

tree. At her feet was a pile of parchments; she was taking a break from reading about several of the proposed solutions to an outbreak of tiny white insects that were currently threatening the papaya crop in the western half of the country.

"He was too scared of her threats at first to admit it," said Rivka, "but then Isaac got close to him and he panicked. I can't understand it."

"I was just trying to be the nice one," said Isaac innocently.

Rivka squinted at him in the sunlight.

"So Dafna's at the root of all this?" said the queen.

Rivka nodded. "Yes. Caleb spilled everything, even things we weren't asking. He started by stealing from Zev—he confessed to that—and then, Dafna caught him trying to steal from Gershom. She filled his head full of threats."

"She said she was a witch and she'd make him bleed from his ears and nose instantly if he told anyone about her or tried to steal from Gershom again," said Isaac. "As if that woman ever had a magical idea. In a gefilte fish, I've sensed more magical training than in her." He snorted at the thought.

"She must have stolen whatever she sold him from someone else," said Shulamit. "Or found it, or... bought it."

"When she caught him stealing, she offered to sell him her special potion," Rivka continued. "He paid for it with what he'd already stolen from Zev."

Shulamit nodded, her eyes narrowing. "We need that potion. We need to stop this. Confiscate it, and bring Dafna here. Maybe now we'll finally find out who impersonated Esther and get her violin back."

♫

115

A team of guards led by Isaac approached Dafna's stall. Since the form of her ill-gotten magic was uncertain, Isaac kept her in his sight even before they'd come close enough to speak to her. Fear flashed into her face for a moment, but she quickly wiped it away and covered it with bravado. "So many attractive guards," she quipped when they got closer. "I'm glad I bothered with scented hair barrettes."

"I thought I smelled trouble," Isaac shot back smoothly.

"Well, trouble's all in how you—"

"Dafna, I think you know why we're here," interrupted the wizard. "Let's not waste time."

Dafna shook her head. "As far as I know, you're all here to buy soap, like everyone else."

"That's not all you're selling here." Isaac gestured to her merchandise. "You have something in this stall with magical properties. Surrender it freely, and Her Majesty may be persuaded to let you keep your permission to sell in the market."

"Wha—magic? Me? If I had magic, do you think I'd be standing up here all day? I'd be sitting by the river eating bourekas!" Dafna laughed, but Isaac saw the nervousness in the set of her jaw.

He signaled with his good hand, and two guards stepped forward and railroaded Dafna out in front of her stall. "Wha—Get off me! You have no right!"

"Make sure she doesn't run off," Isaac ordered, and he entered the stall to begin his search.

"You can't do this! I've done nothing wrong." Dafna's voice carried. "You're interfering with my business. I know—he's going to plant something on me. Gershom!"

"Don't let him get away, either," Isaac called over his shoulder as he saw Gershom emerge from the stall next door. Dafna's shop was a hive of drawers, boxes, baskets, and bags, and each one radiated its own fragrance. The resulting confusion left him feeling as if he were drowning in soap, and he paused for a moment to create a spell that surrounded him with a clean atmosphere.

He sensed the presence of something powerful yet dormant nearby, but in the cascade of ointment bottles and cakes of soap, it was difficult to tell which of so many tiny objects was the key to all the palace's problems of late. A group of intricately carved flasks attracted his attention, but upon poking at them with his own aura, he found them to be nothing more than artwork.

"My husband will appeal to the queen on my behalf, and she'll have you all shoveling horse dung!" Dafna's voice rang loudly from the street. Isaac also heard Gershom's voice, audible but indistinct, muttering at the guards.

"You speak in horse dung," Isaac grumbled. He was carefully, painstakingly, running one finger over every single cake of soap. He was pursuing an idea.

"—foreigner, come in here and—"

Rose, jasmine, litchi... each cake of soap looking just like the rest. Pear, fig—*wait*. There it was.

He passed his right palm over the cake of soap, drawing magic from the unassuming cream-colored block. A vibration rocked his hand, and the soap glowed slightly. When he turned his hand over, he saw that for about three seconds, his scar receded and melted away into his skin, as if it had healed properly. As he watched, the scar returned.

He picked up the soap with his left hand and inspected it. A tiny crack even smaller than a hair showed the place where it had been sliced in half and then sealed shut again with water.

"Bring me water," he called to one of the guards as he stepped out into the street.

When Dafna saw what he had in his hand, she shot Gershom a frightened look. "He's stealing my merchandise!"

A small crowd had gathered from all of her hollering, including Aviva, watching intently with her arms full of carrots, and Micah, whom Isaac noticed hiding in the crawlspace between Dafna's stall and the side she didn't share with Gershom. Likely summoned at the word *stealing*, one of the marketplace officials stalked up to the center of the action and demanded to know what was going on.

"We're here on orders of the queen," Isaac explained calmly.

"I'm sorry, I didn't realize it was law enforcement," said the official. "She was screaming as if she were being knocked over by hooligans."

"They *are* hooligans! Power-hungry—" Dafna fell into invective.

"This is probably just a misunderstand—" Gershom was still trying to weasel out of it.

"Water," said one of the guards, handing Isaac a jug.

Placing the cake of fig-scented soap in his right hand, and careful to stand over the street where he wouldn't damage anything, Isaac poured the water onto the soap. It splashed freely onto the stones as it dripped off his hand.

"What's he doing?" someone in the crowd wanted to know.

"He's crazy."

"No, I think I get it."

Isaac set the jug down on Dafna's table. Then, with his good hand, he pressed against the soap firmly. Drawing on the hidden magic as he had before, he borrowed its power briefly so that he could use his right hand as leverage in the opposite direction.

The two halves of the soap slid apart, and he opened them.

With a half of the soap in each hand, he turned to face Dafna. "Where did you get this stone?"

There was a murmur in the crowd when they saw the black-purple gem that lay inside the hollow of one of the halves.

"It's rightfully mine!" Dafna shot back. Gershom looked uncomfortable.

Aviva stepped closer to peer at it. "It's beautiful. What is it?"

"It's for transformation," Isaac explained quietly. "It merges with the body of the one who swallows it, and changes that person into the self they should be."

"A ripening crystal," Aviva commented.

"You could look at it that way, yes," said Isaac.

"It's the color of ripe figs, anyway."

"That must be why she chose the fig scent to hide it in—so she wouldn't forget where it was." Isaac turned to Dafna. "Where did you get this?"

"It's mine, rightly and legally," Dafna insisted. "Last year I often visited the silk merchant's mother when she was dying of her illness. My scents brought her comfort, and she needed my ointments for her sore body. She gave that stone to me in gratitude for my comforts."

"Well, she would have had no right to do that," Isaac replied. "And I remember her well, and I don't know if I'd be so sure to insist she 'gave' it to you freely."

"After all I did for her—"

119

"Yes, I bet you think you deserved it. Guards—take her to the palace. There are other layers to this," Isaac reminded them.

"But my wares!" Dafna sent a panicked look flying around her shop.

"The guards will pack them up and take them with us," said Isaac. "It wouldn't hurt to examine them all again in case you chose to reward yourself with more of your friend's property."

Chapter 15: The Crystal

Shulamit studied the crystal, watching the sun play off dozens of facets. The light brought out the rich purple, which shadows reduced to only black. "So this—*this*—is what's behind it all? Caleb, Gershom, and the violin?"

Isaac nodded. "Very likely all three, although she hasn't confessed everything yet."

"How does it work?"

"It's intended for one-time use," said Isaac, "created for the sole purpose of permanently transforming a person into their true self."

"Then how are all these people using it to play dress-up for a few hours?"

"Dafna didn't know what it was," Isaac explained, "but she found that if she soaked it in spirits, it leached some of its magic into the liquid."

"Oh, so *that's* what she was selling."

"Exactly."

"How'd she ever figure that out?"

"At one point during her time with it, she'd hidden it in wine," said Isaac, "probably because of the color—and then when she drank the wine later and made a flippant wish about the, er, size of her—"

Shulamit giggled. "That must have been a real surprise!"

"So she's been bottling and selling the spirits as shifting potion ever since."

Shulamit shook her head slowly. "Amazing. And totally—
totally—illegal. For exactly this reason." She paused to shift
Naomi around so she could nurse on the other breast. "The
stone's dangerous. What did you do with it?"

"I have it safe," Isaac said, nonchalantly tapping his pocket.

"As soon as this little girl's finished, I'll go in there and try to
persuade her to tell us who else she sold the potion to besides
Gershom and Caleb." Shulamit rocked Naomi slightly. "How is
Caleb, by the way?"

"He'll be fine," said Isaac. "He's recovered completely from
Riv's temper, and as far as his criminal career—he seems
sufficiently scared of us that I think we can return him to his aunt.
He's still very young."

"Tell his aunt," mused Shulamit, "tell his aunt that as a condition
of his release, he must be apprenticed to someone immediately in
a very lucrative field. He's not a violent person, but he *is* greedy.
If he could direct his energy toward something where he felt like
honest work was financially worth it—"

"I agree," said Isaac. "Hard to see the value of honest work when
honest work is to crush fruit with a pestle all day! For someone
like him, anyway."

"And promise him that Riv will come looking for him if he
strays from an honest path."

"Oh, I will." Isaac winked at her.

♫

With the infant princess sleeping strapped to her chest, Shulamit
crossed the palace to the room where they were holding Dafna.
On the way, she and Rivka had to walk through the area where
the guards had piled all of Dafna's confiscated wares, and the
mixed-up and disturbed scents filled the air. "Phew!" the queen
murmured, careful not to disturb Naomi. "Kind of funny to think

about how, in small amounts, this stuff makes you clean, but a lot of it's almost something you have to go and get clean *from*!"

"Soap doesn't *have* to have scent," was her bodyguard's response.

When they reached Dafna, she was sitting at the simple table behind a cup of water provided by the guards. From its level, it didn't look as though she'd touched much of it. Shulamit perceived discomfort and agitation in her body language, but Dafna's face was a fair attempt at a mask of calm hospitality. *Ever the saleswoman*, she observed.

"Good morning, Your Majesty," said Dafna in a hushed voice. "Your little one's so cute. I remember when mine were that age. I don't want to think about how long ago that's been!" She smiled, but it was strained. "You know, you remind me of one of my daughters. She's always wearing violet, just like you. Likes pretty clothes. They both do."

Rivka remained standing as Shulamit sat down across the table from her, not distracted by the conversational bait. "Dafna," Shulamit began. "We need to talk about the stone."

"It's neat, isn't it? It's really just a beauty aid. I sell beauty aids. I've got powder that can draw attention to your eyes; creams to smooth your skin, wax for your eyebrows—" Dafna must have realized it was the wrong thing to say from the blast of cold air Shulamit could feel coming out of her face, because she quickly backed off. "Not that you need any—Your Majesty—I'm sure you understand, though. Plenty of women come into my shop every day looking for creams, ointments, anything to make their skin healthier or their hair shiny. Is it all that different to do it with magic? I mean, when you think about it, the stuff we get from plants seems like magic anyway."

"It's very different, Dafna, and you know that," said Shulamit quietly.

"It's hard out there when you have these children, growing up, ordering the finest fabrics from the tailor and needing tutors and trips to the Sugar Coast with their friends..." Dafna sighed. "I can't say no to them."

"That doesn't mean you get to break the law so that your kids can go to the beach. That's not how it works," said Shulamit. "The law is there for a reason."

"It's not really a fair law, though, is it?" Dafna replied. "Why should only people with magical training be allowed to use it?"

"They wouldn't be allowed to do illegal things with it, either," said Shulamit. "But with trained wizards, at least we know who they are. People like Isaac and the Queen of the Clay City—wizards always know other wizards. So if someone is using shapeshifting magic to impersonate someone else and commit crimes, we'd have a very small and finite pool of suspects. The minute something like that, human impersonation, sneaks out into the general population—that's a problem. It's a problem for me because I'm in charge of this nation, and it's a problem for Captain Riv because it's his job to protect it. I don't like it when *I* have a problem, and *nobody* likes it when *he* has a problem. As I'm sure you've heard."

"He bought my soap the other day for his mother," Dafna murmured, as if that were some kind of defense.

"Is it maybe a miracle that she didn't turn purple when she used it?" Rivka barked in response.

"That's not fair," Dafna pleaded. "My wares are good quality. It's just a beauty aid, and I can't be held accountable for whatever trouble people got into if they used it for something illegal. I'm not the one who did anything!"

"Shhhh," said both the queen and her captain, and Dafna shot a frightened look at the baby. Luckily, Naomi was still asleep.

124

"I want you to picture something, Dafna," Shulamit began, taking a deep breath. "A young woman, dressed in fine, expensive violet clothing, is safe in her own home... at night." She spoke deliberately, purposely building drama. "A man walks up to her who is closer to her than any other man. This is a man she trusts and looks up to. A man around whom she feels completely and utterly safe." Tightening her embrace around Naomi protectively, she continued. "But it isn't really him, and in the supposed safety of her own home, he lures her into the darkness and assaults her."

In her wide-eyed shock, Dafna knocked over the water. "What? But—Majesty! Last night—he didn't—the guards were saying that young man was going free on probation. They wouldn't—He didn't—" Her expression was utter confusion.

"I wasn't talking about myself and last night," explained the queen. "I was talking about your daughters."

"What?"

"That's what your potion could be used for," said Shulamit. "Think about it. Someone buys it and then uses it to transform into your husband to get inside your house. Your girls. Think about it. With that on the market, I have a major security problem in Home City. Really—*nobody* is safe!"

All the energy had drained from Dafna's face. "Oh my God."

Shulamit waited.

"I knew none of the people I sold it to were going to do anything like that." But she still looked uneasy, and her eyes moved around as though she was wrapping her mind around new ideas.

"How can you really know that about anyone?"

"Well, I mean, not Gershom! We've been friends for years and according to him, he's not interested in sex or romance at all," said Dafna. "He's just not built like that. So he would never—"

Shulamit looked at Rivka. She'd caught it too. "Gershom wanted it to steal Zev's designs, didn't he?"

Dafna bit her lip.

"Come on, Dafna. It'll be easier for you this way. I'm sure you don't want the hassle of having your marketplace license taken away."

"He wasn't going to hurt anyone," she insisted. "But, yes. He did sneak into Zev's workshop."

"Thank you," said Shulamit. "What about Caleb? He's not even from here. How could you know he wasn't going to attack me?"

"Oh, him!" Dafna said dismissively. "That one's not violent at all. He's just after easy money."

"That's still not your call to make," said Shulamit. "Dafna, if all the thing did was get rid of wrinkles for a few hours, or make your body more shapely, I'd be all for it. It wouldn't be dangerous—although I wish people didn't feel they had to do things like that. I wish *I* didn't feel pressure to do things like that. But it's far more than that and can cause a whole lot of trouble. Now, I have to ask you about who else bought the potion. Unless Gershom had something to do with the stolen violin?"

"No, not that I know of," said Dafna. "He only bought the one lot."

"Well?" Shulamit threw up one free hand, the one not supporting the baby. "Then are you going to tell me who else bought it?"

Chapter 16: Borrowed Wings That Flew Too High

Esther lingered in the street outside Tzuriel's shop. Her mouth felt sticky and uncomfortable. The only lunch she'd been able to stomach had been a banana yogurt drink, and her nerves made her over-aware of its unpleasant remnants. Dawdling, she looked around at the other stalls. Her gaze rested briefly on the jewelry seller across the path. She thought about killing time in there, losing herself in more trifling over meaningless products. It was silly; she'd already bought presents for her mother and sisters, and she had no great desire for any more jewelry for herself at the moment. No, she needed to stop putting it off.

Nervously, she entered the shop.

It was a busy day for Tzuriel, who was juggling his attention between two parties of customers—but he still found space in his attention for her. As soon as she entered the shop, he turned toward her and flashed her a huge smile. "Hey!"

"Afternoon," she said through a smile she hadn't intended to release and looked away quickly.

"Aba! Aba! Look at this one!" A tiny girl was practically jumping up and down as she tugged her father's arm, pointing with the other hand at a group of brightly painted wooden flutes. "It matches my everything!"

"I don't know if that one's too big for you, Kitten," said her father. He looked up with questioning eyes at Tzuriel, who was still helping a group of strong-looking young men pick out drums.

"It's okay," said one of the young men. "You can help them— we'd like a few moments to try these out."

"Go for it!" Tzuriel held out his hand invitingly. "Just don't go full tilt, or all the other shops on the block will have my head." He walked up to the little girl and her father.

Esther tried to disappear into the jumble of the shop's wares, quietly plucking open strings on a psalter resting on a corner shelf.

"I don't want to settle on that one right away," said the father under his voice when Tzuriel was close enough that he could speak to him without his daughter hearing. "Five minutes ago she was jumping for joy over violins. And yesterday, all she would talk about was the trumpet."

"She's just excited about music in general." Tzuriel looked at the little girl, happily looking at the flutes, and smiled broadly. "It's great to see that, at her age."

Esther was watching, entranced, in spite of herself, thinking of her little sisters. Home felt far away, and yet the images comforted her.

"So should I just choose for her?" The father looked around at everything, clearly bewildered at the variety. Drumbeats from the young men at the other end of the shop punctuated his puzzled silence. "Can you help me pick something out?"

"How about I tell you about each instrument," suggested Tzuriel, "so that you'll feel better about deciding on your own?"

"Sure, if you have the time!"

Tzuriel waved at the other customers dismissively. "They're enjoying themselves on those drums. They're fine."

"I guess I'd rather she not get drums, or my wife and I will live with constant headaches."

"Not really," said Tzuriel. "There are quieter drums. Listen to this—gentle as a cat's footsteps at midnight." With just his fingertips, he beat a fluttering rhythm on a tiny drum no bigger than a grapefruit.

"I don't want that one," said the little girl.

"It's important that she has something she likes," Tzuriel pointed out. "Otherwise, kids that age, they won't practice."

"She's so young, I don't know if she'll practice as it is," murmured the father.

"If it's the right one for her, she will," said Tzuriel with a smile. "Esther, you were her age when you started on violin, weren't you?"

Esther, who'd almost forgotten they could see her, blinked rapidly and nodded. "Yes, a very tiny one!"

"You have to start on a smaller instrument. They can't hold the adult ones at that age," Tzuriel explained.

"How does the violin work?" asked the father. "I've heard beginners before, and they sound like dying mice. I don't know if I could live with that."

"There are really two pieces—the bow, and the violin," said Tzuriel. "Esther can probably explain it better than I can."

"Well, there are three ways you can change the way your note sounds, on a violin," said Esther, directing her voice at the little girl. "How heavily you press down with the bow on the strings, how fast you move your bow arm, and whether the bow is near to you or farther away. A lot of beginners make a funny noise just because they don't press down hard enough for the speed of their arm."

"That sounds really complicated," said the little girl, wide-eyed.

"You get used to it," said Esther. "I really was just your size when I started."

"Is flute easier?"

"It's usually thought to be easier," said Tzuriel. "But you can only play one note at a time." He cast a look at Esther, tossing her the conversational ball.

"That's right. Whereas, if I'm all by myself, I can be my own accompaniment."

"Are there instruments where I can play by myself that are easier than violin?" asked the little girl.

"Let me show you the dulcimer," said Tzuriel, leading them over to a shelf.

"It has strings like a violin," the little girl observed.

"But instead of a bow, you use little hammers to play them." Tzuriel fished around for a matching set. "Like this." He began to demonstrate, and Esther felt her bones moving in time to the rhythm.

"I really like that one!" The little girl looked up at her father.

"Are you sure?" asked the father cautiously.

"You can play by yourself, but you can also play with other people," Tzuriel pointed out. "Esther, grab a fiddle off the wall."

"What?"

"Come on! Let's show her what she can do."

Eyelashes fluttering again, she crossed to the wall and picked up the closest violin. Tightening the bow with familiar, automatic movements made her feel as though she'd been given air again after days in stuffy smoke. She lifted the alien fiddle to her shoulder. It was too thin and too shrill, but *God* if it didn't feel good to have wings again. Even if they weren't the right wings and didn't fit properly.

She toyed around with the chords that Tzuriel played until she could find the melody—always tricky to do with an instrument that plays so much of its own accompaniment underneath—and then launched into it full-force.

The little girl began to dance and twirl around, giggling madly. Then the men on the drums stopped fooling around and listened. Soon, they too joined in. Esther leaned into the instrument, tossing her hair, her hips moving in time.

Tzuriel motioned with his head, beckoning for the little girl to approach. Soon, he had the hammers in her hands, and, under the watchful eye of her father, he guided her hands over the strings. "I can do this!"

"Sure you can!" he agreed.

As Esther wound her phrase to a close and put the fiddle away, the girl came bounding up to her. "You sounded great! How did I do?"

"You're gonna do great," said Esther, and the girl beamed.

"Will she be able to come back to you for lessons?" asked the father.

"No, I'm not always here," said Tzuriel. "I travel." Esther felt heat creep into her face. "But I can give you the names of all the local musicians. The dulcimer, then?"

"And the little sticks."

"Hammers."

"If you say so!"

Esther sank back into the shadowed corner as they politely haggled over the price. Tzuriel's attention was captured by the drummers after the father and daughter's departure, and she used the time to clear her head and pray.

131

When they, too, were on their way out, she took a deep breath and readied herself. As she drew out of the shadows, the last of the drummers turned around and called to her, "Thanks for the music—that was world class!"

"Thanks," she called after them.

And then they left, and just as simple as that, the shop was empty except for her and Tzuriel.

"Hi," he said.

"Hi."

"We make a good team. That was almost magical."

"What was that tune?"

"Little something I made up," said Tzuriel. "I call it 'Sugar Coast Ramblin'.'"

"You miss your home?"

"I don't have time to miss anything—but I love it, and I go back when I can. Have you ever been?"

Esther shook her head. "Someday, I'd like to."

"Anyway, I really appreciate your help today. That little girl will always remember the story of how she got her dulcimer."

"She reminds me of my baby sisters," said Esther, a little misty. Then she exhaled in the flavor of a laugh. "They're so much older than that, now. Sixteen and thirteen." Wearing grownup clothing, and so far away from the enthusiastic little girls who at nine and six years old had painted garish butterflies on her violin case.

"I bet they look up to you a lot."

"Yes, my family is very proud." Esther took a step closer, her heart beating so heavily that her stomach felt as if she'd eaten it.

She took something out of her bag. "Tzuriel, thank you for loaning me the kalimba." The words *I don't want Eli to find it* floated through her head, but she didn't say them. "I'm glad to have had it for a little while, but..."

"It's a gift, yours to keep." Tzuriel reached out his fingers, but he didn't take the kalimba—instead, he took Esther's hand in his. She began to tremble. Tzuriel took a step closer. "Esther, you've captured my heart. Your talents, your sweetness, your conversation—how many reasons does a man need to fall in love? Hearing you join in when I was playing that dulcimer felt like strings finally playing in tune. Come with me, play music with me—let's share music and fellowship together, everywhere we go."

Esther let out a squeak like a goose, then cleared her throat. She knew she wanted him to kiss her, but the whole *point* of this was—"These past few days—without my violin—I can really see how important Eli is to me. Especially away from my family like this. I think you're... a really good guy, and I love watching you work. But Eli is my other constant, beside music, and he deserves my loyalty after all he's done for me."

"But does he understand your music?"

"Does that matter?" Esther asked. "I don't even have it right now."

"Your music will never leave you. God will make sure of that."

"At some point I need to go home and give him the life he deserves."

"Why do *you* deserve that?"

"I—" Her chest heaved with passion and confusion. She thought of Eli needing her and of her own selfishness, how he was here with her in Home City instead of back home studying law as he wanted—even though it had been his idea to come with her—how

133

she'd driven him miserable fretting over a piece of wood which wasn't even alive. "I don't deserve anything."

"You are the *most* deserving."

"Someone's coming!"

"Hm?" Tzuriel turned around, and from behind him Esther saw two of the royal guards approaching, one older, one younger.

"Tzuriel ben Kofi?" asked the older one.

"That's me."

"We're here to arrest you for the theft of the historical violin," said the guard.

"What?" Tzuriel's face broke into a surprised smile. "No."

Esther's face grew hot. "What's going on?"

"Pack all this up and put it in the wagon," the older guard directed the younger one. Esther peered outside and saw more guards, and even horses. "The queen will want to search it. You, come with us." He tried to take Tzuriel by the wrist.

"I didn't take her violin," Tzuriel protested.

"You were identified by the woman who sold you the shapeshifting tonic," the guard replied flatly.

"Tzuriel!" Esther cried, her eyes a distraught plea.

"Sorry, young lady," said the guard. "You have to be careful, you know, being a young woman all on your own. Some of these men—"

Esther wrapped Eli's blue scarf around her shoulders and burst into tears as they led Tzuriel out into the street.

Chapter 17: The Fat Man

"Your Majesty, Tzuriel ben Kofi is in the prison cell," said Tivon, bowing.

"Thank you," said Shulamit. She was pacing around her throne room, the baby strapped to her chest. Rivka remained beside the throne. "What about the instruments from his shop?"

"We brought them all back in the wagon like you asked," Tivon replied.

"I hope you were careful with them. Some of those things are pretty delicate."

"We did everything we could."

"Thank you. I'll go out and look at them in a minute. Dismissed."

Aviva appeared in the doorway, almost colliding with Tivon as he exited. "Here's a little kiss for your stomach." She handed Shulamit a dish of sliced mangoes, and the queen rewarded her with a kiss on the cheek. "What's going on? Why is there a music shop in the outer courtyard?"

"It's all of Tzuriel's merchandise," said Shulamit. "Apparently he's the one who bought shapeshifting magic from Dafna, so the violin must be among his wares."

"Unless he already sold it," Rivka pointed out. "He's a dealer."

"Right."

Aviva shook her head. "No way. Not him."

Shulamit shrugged, chewing fruit. "That's what Dafna said, anyway. And he *was* one of our three suspects."

135

"I've got herbs to chop," said Aviva. "See you at dinner."

"Looking forward to it!" said Shulamit. "Maybe this whole thing will be solved by then!"

But the afternoon's search of the contents of the wagon proved fruitless, and both Shulamit and Isaac spent several hours baking in the direct sunlight to no avail. There wasn't anywhere within the palace courtyard that was both big enough to hold a large wagon and yet fully shaded, and Perach was very sunny. By the time she'd satisfied herself that none of the violins were Esther's, and he could verify that none of the other instruments were violins bewitched to look like trumpets, or hiding tiny, temporarily shrunken violins inside their cavities, they were both uncomfortable and thirsty.

"Uggh. I'm going to go jump in the creek and change my clothes before I question Tzuriel."

"I can take Naomi, if you want," Isaac offered. "I will just crack open a coconut."

Several hours later, in the little kitchen-house, Aviva placed a dish of spicy lamb kebabs in the center of the table. She was beaming as usual, an unnoticed piece of carrot peel stuck in her hair.

"This looks fantastic," said Shulamit eagerly, helping herself from the dish. "And I can't wait to eat. I've just about memorized those pest control briefs, and I still don't know what happened to that violin!"

"How did the questions go?" asked Isaac.

Shulamit grimaced. "He swears up and down he had nothing to do with it, that he'd never hurt Esther, that he's never bought anything from Dafna—actually, he said he's never even seen Dafna. He said he still has soap with him from the last place he set up shop and hasn't needed anything here yet."

"He can say anything," Rivka pointed out, already wolfing down food. "Whoo! Spicy."

"You northerners," Aviva teased. "Fat, salt, onion." Then she giggled wickedly. "That's why you came down here!"

"I am Riv Maror; I am not to be defeated by a pain in the mouth." Rivka shoveled more of the lamb into her mouth, as if to prove a point.

"She's spicier than the food, anyway," Isaac murmured, and Shulamit saw Rivka sit up even straighter.

"It's not him," said Aviva, finally retrieving the carrot peel from her hair. "I'm telling you."

"Dafna identified him conclusively," Shulamit reminded her.

"Yes, but Dafna is the banana that rots when it's still green," Aviva insisted.

"I know it hurts your feelings when someone in the working class gets accused," said Shulamit, "but every group has dishonest people in it."

"That's not it. Listen to me," Aviva protested. "Tzuriel is a man of the marketplace. They don't leave their spots."

"Then she must have come to him."

"She wouldn't leave her spot, either," said Aviva. "I saw her when Isaac came to take her away. She was very protective of her merchandise. She wouldn't have left her stall unguarded and walked all the way across the market like that. It's not like he's next door, and even if you're next door that's still dangerous. Things have a way of walking off. Everything in a market has legs."

"She's friends with Gershom; she could have asked him to watch the soap."

"He's got a busy shop of his own, and it only takes a thief seconds to sting your ankle. She's been doing this for years, and she knows that just as well as I do."

"Maybe she sent a messenger." But even as Shulamit said the words, she knew they were wrong. "Although that doesn't fit the way she works. She doesn't like getting in trouble, and she'd never approach anyone she didn't already have a feeling would go for it."

"If he didn't take it, why did she say he did?" asked Rivka.

"What exactly did she say, *Malkeleh*?" asked Isaac, a crafty look slipping into his eye.

"She said... that it was the fat man with 'tails' in his hair, tied back," said the queen. "She didn't know his name."

"Does anyone else around here have their hair in locks?" asked Isaac.

"Nobody as big as Tzuriel," said Rivka.

"The locks are a Sugar Coast thing, and all the Sugar Coast people I can think of in the capital are much thinner than he is," said Shulamit.

"And he swears he's never seen her," said Isaac.

"Right." Then Shulamit clapped her hands to her mouth. "If somebody wanted us to *think* it was him—"

"All they'd have to do is tell her to say it was the fat man with that hairstyle," Isaac answered her.

"But he says he never saw her."

"Which means she never saw *him*."

"If he's telling the truth."

"If we had another fat man with locks," Isaac mused, "that we knew didn't do it, we could sneak him in to where she's eating and ask her to identify the man who bought the potion."

"We don't have another fat man from the Sugar Coast," Shulamit pointed out, "but we do have Big Simon. And she'd never recognize him, because he's always on night watch on the treasury." It lay deep within the palace walls, so Big Simon didn't often get out to the marketplace.

"Big Simon is bald," Rivka pointed out.

"So we'll have to get a wig," said Shulamit.

"My father has wigs for his mannequins," Aviva reminded them, "for when he sells clothing at market."

"Are any of them styled into locks?" asked Shulamit.

"No, but maybe Isaac can sing to them."

Shulamit looked at the wizard. "Do you think you could figure out how to...?"

"I'll try!" said Isaac. His eyes twinkled at the prospect of the trickery ahead.

♫

The sun had gone down, so the flurry of activity in Ben's dressmaking studio took place by lamplight. Big Simon stood in the center of the room, waiting patiently for Ben to emerge from the trunk in which he was rummaging. Everybody else was focused on Big Simon, except for Aviva, in the corner playing with Naomi and some toys.

"Try this one," said Ben as he came up for air, a dark brown sherwani jacket in his hands.

"That one looks more like it'll fit." Big Simon took off the green one he was wearing, which hadn't sat properly across his broad form.

"It doesn't have to be comfortable, as long as it covers his guard uniform for a few moments." Rivka circled the room like a prowling wolf.

"Comfortable, no, but it does have to look like he's in his regular clothes," Shulamit reminded her.

"I'm getting overtime for this, right?"

"Yes, definitely," Rivka asserted.

"Looks like this one fits," said Big Simon. "Now what?"

"Now, the wig," said Isaac, his arms folded across his chest. "Ben? What do you have?"

"This is the one I use for male mannequins," said Ben, holding up a mass of black horsehair.

"No, that one's too short."

"Well, here's the lady one." Ben tossed the other one over to Isaac.

The false hair was thick and straight. "I think I can work with this." Isaac turned it over and over in his hands. Before their eyes, the strands began to cluster together, twisting like little cyclones. When he was finished, he held it up. "How's that?"

Shulamit nodded. "Pretty good!" She looked at Rivka.

"Works for me," the captain agreed.

"Okay, put it on." Shulamit carried the wig to Big Simon, who fit it to his big, shining, bald head.

"How do I look?"

Shulamit tried her hardest not to giggle, but her face shattered into laughter despite her best efforts. "Oh, goodness."

"What?" Big Simon stepped in front of the glass where Shulamit usually tried on her new clothes. "Oh! Ho ho." He began to laugh as well. "Who's that handsome face?"

"Tie them back," Shulamit pointed out. "Tzuriel wears his locks tied back." On Tzuriel, they looked natural and, in fact, suave; on her guard... not so much.

"Oh, yeah," said Rivka.

"Here, use this." Ben gave him a ribbon.

"I never had this much hair even when I *had* hair!" Simon fiddled with the ribbon awkwardly, and eventually Ben stepped in to help him.

"Now, you have to pretend we've arrested you this morning—" Shulamit began, but Big Simon was making such silly faces into the mirror that she burst into giggles again. "Stooooop."

"I have so much hair!" Big Simon grinned.

"Please be serious," Shulamit ordered.

"Yes, Majesty. You were saying?"

"You were arrested this morning, and you know you didn't do it, but you're scared, and you're about to face the woman who's accused you—Stop that!" Big Simon was laughing at himself in the mirror again.

Rivka marched up to him. "Listen, you nightcrawling *schmegeggeh*, you can stick your head in the ground and grow upside down like an onion once this drama is over for all I care, but you will *stop laughing* and get in character before I rip that wig off your head and stuff it down your throat."

141

"Sir, yes, sir!" Big Simon was instantly serious, his face a rigid mask and his body a statue.

This time it was Shulamit and Aviva who chuckled, and Isaac's face blossomed into a predictable half-smile of admiration for his wife's sheer power.

When Shulamit had gotten the laughter out of her system, she took one final look at Big Simon and then nodded at Rivka. She and Isaac took up position on either side of him and bound him as if he were a prisoner.

Dafna was in one of the holding cells, finishing her dinner. She rose when she saw the queen's party approaching. "Can I go home yet? My husband will be frantic for me."

"We've sent word," Shulamit reassured her.

Fear flitted into Dafna's face. "You didn't tell him—"

"He knows you're being held at the palace as a witness connected with several thefts," Shulamit replied. "We didn't say you'd done anything wrong yourself, but it may come to that. You still owe us a fine for the illegal use of shapeshifting magic."

Dafna looked around uneasily. "Am I going to be here overnight?"

"Probably," said the queen. "It depends."

"On what?"

Shulamit clapped her hands. It was the signal for Rivka and Isaac to bring their prisoner into the room. "Dafna, do you recognize this man?"

Dafna's face was blank for a moment, and then she must have realized she was looking at a fat man with his hair twisted into locks. When Shulamit saw that spark of recognition in her face, she felt like she'd hooked a fish. Rather than yank up the pole

142

before the bait was swallowed, she waited patiently, thinking of her father and how proud moments like this would have made him.

"That's him, Majesty," said Dafna. "That's the third man who bought my tonic."

"Are you sure? He says he didn't," said Shulamit placidly.

"Oh, well, he can say anything he likes, but I would remember a man like that." Dafna grew more self-possessed as she committed fully to the lie.

"When was this?"

"Oh, I don't know. The day of that big concert, maybe."

Shulamit noticed that Dafna wasn't meeting Big Simon's eyes with her own.

"That's really funny, Dafna," said Shulamit, crossing her arms across her chest, "because this is Big Simon, the night watchman for my treasury. And he doesn't usually leave the palace walls."

Chapter 18: Teeth Begin to Emerge

Dafna's shoulders slumped. She sighed and looked into the corner of the floor.

Shulamit stepped closer. "How about you tell us who told you to tell us that?"

Dafna shook her head sadly. "I don't know his name," she said, and to Shulamit, she finally sounded sincere.

"So it was a man, then?"

"He wasn't fat, and he wasn't light-skinned like those two." Dafna pointed at Isaac and Rivka. "No accent, either. But he spoke in a hushed whisper and he was wearing a lady's veil, so I couldn't see his face."

"And you didn't recognize anything about him?"

"No. Just his coin." Dafna finally looked as though she might be feeling ashamed of herself.

"So he came up to you on the day of the concert, bought the potion, and told you to give us a false lead if you were caught?" Shulamit went over all the facts meticulously.

"No, not exactly." Dafna paused for a moment to collect herself. "The day of the concert, Gershom came back from speaking with you. We talked about whether or not you'd figured us out, and the man in the veil must have been lurking behind the booths. He showed up later, hours after the conversation, but he seemed to have heard everything we'd said. He offered me money right there on the spot, so of course I took it."

"Why didn't you think he was a spy from the palace?" asked Shulamit.

"That's a good question," Dafna admitted. "I don't know."

"She was greedy," suggested Rivka, and Dafna looked embarrassed.

"What about the fat man?" asked Shulamit.

"That was later," said Dafna. "He came back on another day—I don't remember which day—and gave me more money, and told me that if you figured out what I was selling, to say that he was a fat man with his hair like that."

"And he still had the veil on?"

"Yes, Majesty. May I go home yet?" She looked around the cell sadly, seeing the sack of straw on which she'd have to sleep if she remained overnight.

Shulamit nodded. "I think so. You'll pay the fine to the guards when we get you home?"

"Yes, Majesty."

"Do you understand why you can't sell shapeshifting magic anymore?"

"Yes, Majesty." Dafna hung her head.

"Oh, I can take this silly thing off now," realized Big Simon suddenly.

♫

"She's so glad to see you!" Aviva handed the fussy little princess over to Shulamit as the queen entered the comforting womb of the kitchen-house. Rivka was close behind. She sat down at the table and began cracking open peanuts and eating them.

"You mean she's glad to see these." Shulamit gestured wearily at her chest.

"If I could, I would," Aviva reminded her.

"I'm sorry, I'm tired," said Shulamit. "I'm not thinking." She sat down and opened the side of her tunic so that Naomi could latch on.

"Was I right about Tzuriel?" Aviva asked, bending down from behind Shulamit to rub both her upper arms affectionately.

"We set him free. Someone paid Dafna to lie."

Aviva kissed her on the cheek. "I knew you'd get to the truth. It's a good thing you love me anyway—it'd be awfully inconvenient to have a crush on the queen all by myself!"

Shulamit turned her face to the side so that she could kiss her on the mouth. "You've been eating something sweet."

"Dried figs. You want?"

"One or two."

Isaac slipped smoothly into the room, smiled at the girls, and put his hand on Rivka's shoulder in greeting.

"Dafna paid you?" asked Shulamit, looking up at him.

Isaac nodded. "Tivon has the money. He's taking it to the treasury now."

"This is almost over," said Shulamit, "except it's not over at all. We don't know who that man was."

"Well, you ruled out Tzuriel, since the man in the veil wasn't fat," Rivka pointed out. "So funny, isn't it? Here I am in a mask playing a man, and a man walks around in a lady's veil—"

"Wait! Wait—" said Shulamit. "Maybe it wasn't a man!"

"You mean—Liora?" asked Rivka.

"She's really tall, for a woman," Shulamit pointed out.

"Not as tall as I am," Rivka replied.

"You're a giant," said Shulamit.

Isaac made a face like a sleeping cat.

"Dafna did say that he was whispering," continued the queen. "Say it was Liora. Maybe she bought it, but then the marquis was the one who used it."

"Or it was maybe the marquis himself, and he bought it *and* took the potion," Rivka suggested.

"Right. Or our other male suspect—the innkeeper. It's really down to those three at this point, isn't it?" Shulamit paused to arrange Naomi at the other breast. "I keep thinking about that business with trying to frame Tzuriel. He came back the next day to do that."

"Or on a different day." Isaac pointed out. "She didn't say the next day."

"Right," said Shulamit. "So that means the means the frame-up wasn't part of the original plan."

"So then it can't really be the innkeeper," said Isaac.

"No, it can't, because he set up the party in advance," said Shulamit, a slow, full smile spreading across her face. Smiles fit awkwardly onto her bone structure, so it looked a little bit like the hostile grin of a wild animal. Nevertheless, she felt safe with her family in the little kitchen-house, and more free to smile.

"That's it, then!" said Rivka, pounding her fist on the table and making peanut shells dance around. "It's either the marquis going behind Liora's back, or it's the two of them together." She stood up. "You want I should go arrest them?"

147

"No, no, sit down, Riv." Shulamit watched her captain retake her chair slowly, reminding her of a snake pulling back into its coil. "I want Isaac to go sneaking around as a lizard, to see if he can sniff up any trace of the violin in their villa. Getting that silly thing back intact is the most important thing to me, at this point. We've already caught two thieves and a...whatever Dafna is. Now that we have only one place to search, it'll be easier."

"You're so sexy when I can see your brilliant mind reflecting like sun on the water like that." Aviva beamed.

"Not half as sexy as you are when you're standing up for the honest working person," Shulamit shot back.

"That's the tree where I sprouted," Aviva said smoothly, "and I'm still in its branches, really..." She looked around the kitchen-house where she spent so much time, toiling on foods that would bring joy to her family and keep the queen out of sickbed.

"You're such a special woman." Shulamit gazed at her adoringly. "So many people... royalty falls in love with them, they'd take it as an opportunity to seize a life of luxury."

"Didn't you used to fear that living with the love of another woman counted as a luxury?" Aviva pointed out. "I have a family. That's my silk cushion. Besides," she added with a jut of her hip, "I have enough cushion to sit on."

"If you ever sit down at all! I love how you're always dreaming up new projects..."

"That reminds me—the wheat-free challah was a success, right?"

"It meant the world to me. You know that."

"I think I might make some extra this week, and sell it to one of the bakers in the marketplace." Aviva brushed a loose wisp of hair out of her face. "For anyone else in Home City with your issues."

148

"What a fantastic idea! Oh, Aviva, maybe someday they'll tell legends of you..."

"See, Princess Naomi?" Isaac interjected, speaking to the groggy little baby. "That's true love. Your mothers are proud of each other and support each other in their great ideas. Nobody's jealous and wants the other one to stay home with her all the time."

"You'd know all about that, wouldn't you, Wizard?" quipped Rivka.

"Do you remember the man who would have wanted *you* to stay home and have his babies? You of all people."

"The general?" Rivka laughed. "I wish I could now meet him in battle."

"Isaac..." Shulamit interrupted them. "I've had another idea. Would you mind looking in two places tonight?

♫

When Isaac returned to the palace, it was only a few hours before dawn. He expected everyone to be in bed except the night guards, but on his way back to the quarters he shared with Rivka, he saw lamplight flickering from an open doorway. Within seconds, he heard the distressed wail of an infant and knew why there was still activity in the royal wing.

He slipped inside the room, which was Mitzi's. "What's wrong?"

"Her first tooth is starting to... tooth." Shulamit looked bleary and overcooked.

Meanwhile, Mitzi was rocking Naomi back and forth, singing to her softly in her native tongue. A bottle of wine stood open on an end table.

"On the bottom." Rivka gestured on her own mouth.

149

"She woke up and wouldn't go back to sleep," said Shulamit. "She's in too much pain."

"*Mammeh* was still up, so I figured she'd know what to do."

"Shh..." Mitzi walked over to Rivka. "Can you put please some more wine on my finger?"

Rivka helped her mother get a fingerful of wine, which she proceeded to rub across the baby's sore gums. "Is that really enough to numb her?"

"It might," said Mitzi. "We did this with you, back years ago."

"Here's the string of amber beads from Queen Aafsaneh." Rivka offered them to her mother.

"Oh, I was wondering where those were," said the queen.

"Majesty, I can take her through the night if you want to sleep," Mitzi offered. "I've done this before. Isaac, you should have seen when Rivka was this age. No matter how much it got me in trouble with my brother and his wife, she wailed for a week solid. Meanwhile, all his girls, they were quiet even when they were fretful."

"Rivka's not a quiet soul," said Isaac evenly.

Shulamit yawned. "If you're sure. Thank you, Mitzi." She walked out into the hallway, and Isaac followed. "What did you find?"

He showed her what he was holding in his left hand, and she looked up at him with studious eyes.

"What about...?"

He shook his head. "No."

"Where was it?"

She listened as he told her. There was more, and she received the news solemnly.

"Very well. Gather everyone together in the morning—"

"Everyone? Not just—"

"No, everyone involved. For some of those people, having their name cleared will be very important."

"And what about the crown?"

"The crown will see justice served. But for now, the crown is going back to bed."

Chapter 19: A Summons to Breakfast

Esther was washing her face in the basin the next morning when she heard the knock. "I'm sorry, I'm almost ready," she called to Eli.

It wasn't Eli. "The palace guards are here," said the innkeeper from the other side of the door. "The queen's summoned us all for breakfast."

"What? Oh, okay." Puzzled, Esther dried her face on a linen towel. She felt among the dresses she'd washed the night before for one that had dried completely. Perhaps the queen was summoning her to the palace to collect her violin, finally retrieved from wherever Tzuriel had hidden it, but then why invite the innkeeper? Who was "us all," anyway?

Eli was waiting for her in the courtyard with the innkeeper. "What's all this about?" he asked.

"I don't know, but maybe I'll finally get my violin back."

"I hope you'd worry this much about me, if I were missing."

"You know I would."

The guards, who had been waiting patiently, beckoned to them. "All three of you, please come with us," said the one with a great big beard.

The early morning air was pleasant and cool, not like the heat of day, and Esther looked upon the bustle of the marketplace setting itself up as they skirted its outer rim. Birds chirped in the trees, and a breeze picked up the edges of her filmy clothing and made it dance around. She felt in the sweet smell of morning that everything was going to be all right soon.

The first time she'd seen the palace, the morning after the theft when she was questioned, she'd been too distressed to notice its beauty. Tall palms rose like sentinels on either side of the great gates, and inside the walls, the white, gleaming houses reposed against the backdrop of the lush gardens, capped with curving tiles of red clay. There were other grand buildings in the capital with similar design, but none so fine, so lavish, so immaculately clean.

Once inside, the guards showed them into a large reception area. Liora was already there, on the arm of the marquis, and she approached Esther as soon as she saw her. "Good morning! Any word on your fiddle yet? I have no idea why we're here. It's a good thing I was up and dressed already when the guards showed up. Getting in some extra practicing—I'm leaving on tour myself, soon. I have new tunes I want to introduce to the world."

"I haven't heard anything yet, but I guess that's why we're here." Esther looked around. Besides herself and Eli and the innkeeper, there were Liora and her marquis and also the street youth— Micah. She was startled to see Tzuriel, but there were guards everywhere and she figured the queen had something up her sleeve. He shot her a look full of meaning, but she didn't meet his eye.

There were covered dishes on a table at the side of the room, and cushions had been set up on the floor. Esther didn't feel comfortable touching anything in the royal setting until she was told to, however, and everyone else seemed to feel the same way.

"Her Majesty Queen Shulamit," announced one of the guards.

In walked the rose-clad queen with the infant princess strapped to her chest, followed by her foreign bodyguard. The wizard was the last to enter the room, and he remained in the background.

The company bowed. "Thank you for coming, everyone," said Queen Shulamit. "I've had them offer breakfast for you all." The guards removed the covers from the dishes, and Esther saw bread that had been dredged in egg and covered with sugar. "Please, eat!"

"But we must wait for you, Majesty," the marquis reminded her.

"Oh, I've already eaten," said the queen pleasantly. "Believe me, I'd love to join you, but if I ate that, I'd get sick."

"My dear Majesty," said the marquis, "if you only gave up this nonsense about wheat, your life would be so much easier."

Captain Riv bounded across the room in two paces until he was nose to nose with the marquis. "Wheat is for her literally *poison*, you uncompassionate *schmegeggeh*. Like your attitude on my ears. She provides for you this breakfast, and you—"

"Riv." Shulamit, smiling, held up one hand. "Thank you. Marquis, I'd love to eat that. I really would. I just love not having stomach cramps more." The baby fussed, and Shulamit adjusted her in the wrap. "Sorry, she's teething. Seriously, eat."

Micah didn't need to be commanded, and was already heaping the sweetened toast on a plate. Esther, still a bit puzzled by the strange collection of people in the room, including Tzuriel, wound up farther back in the line than she'd intended to.

While they were arranging themselves on the cushions, one of the guards brought in a chair for Queen Shulamit. She sat, kissing her baby's forehead and murmuring soothing words.

"Everyone is fed, Majesty," pointed out another guard.

"Thank you," said Queen Shulamit. Then, addressing her guests, she began, "As a result of yesterday's adventures, we now know that Esther's violin was stolen with the aid of a shapeshifting potion."

There was a general gasping among her audience. "Wizards!" grumped the innkeeper, and Esther saw him glaring at Isaac.

154

"Isaac had nothing to do with it," Queen Shulamit interjected. "He's loyal to me and therefore to the law of my throne, and he would never sell anything that would cause that much trouble for keeping the peace." She paused to take a breath. "Someone obtained the potion through an illicit source that has since been neutralized, left the room during the innkeeper's dinner, and then reentered it in the guise of a servant headed through the inner courtyard towards the kitchen. Then, while hidden in the curtains that shield the doorway, the disguise was changed to that of Esther herself. That was how the rabbi and the two women saw nobody but Esther enter her room during the dinner."

Esther looked around the room in bewilderment. Someone had pretended to be her?

"We originally thought it was Tzuriel," the queen continued, "but that was determined to be a lie resulting from a bribe." She studied the faces of the group as if looking for a reaction. "Besides, we searched his wares and he didn't have the instrument."

"He's a dealer," the innkeeper called out quickly. "He could have sold it already."

Queen Shulamit shook her head. "It wasn't him. The person selling the potion had never even seen him. So I was down to one of the rest of you. I thought I'd ruled you out, actually, because if you'd wanted to frame Tzuriel, you could have set up the bribe from the beginning, since you knew he was coming to the party."

"What do you mean, you *thought* you ruled me out?" The innkeeper's brow furrowed.

"Well, then I realized—" She paused. "If you and Tzuriel were working together, then you could have bought the potion and then double-crossed him the next day. By that time, you'd already have the money from him buying it from you, and he'd be the one found with the violin. In a way, it's almost kind, at least to Esther, because it puts the instrument back in her hands."

155

"But it's not true!" the innkeeper protested, standing up and looking around him.

"I know that, so please sit down," ordered the queen.

Confused, and looking irritated but pacified, the innkeeper sat. He glared at everyone else suspiciously.

"Marquis, it would have been awfully convenient for you if Esther's violin had gone missing," Queen Shulamit continued. "I know it's not true, but everyone thinks of Esther as Liora's competition, and without Esther's violin, Liora could get publicity raising money for a new one. You may even have been able to benefit from selling her the other expensive violin. You have a lot of motives."

"You must think I have a lot of patience too," said the marquis petulantly.

"Relax, she knows we had nothing to do with it." Liora patted his arm gently. Then, under her breath, Esther heard her add, "And you don't want to get Captain Riv mad at you again."

"Do I?" Shulamit asked. "The one who bought the potion could have been you. You're tall, for a woman, so you could have pretended to be a man—in the right clothes."

Liora simply looked at her without saying anything.

"But... it wasn't you two, either." The infant princess was fussing again, and then started to cry outright. The queen looked distressed.

"I'll take her." Isaac dove in and collected the baby. He walked her back and forth and let her chew on something he was holding. Esther couldn't help but follow him with her eyes. She'd been a little bit scared of him ever since their first meeting, but seeing him in such a kindly role—this was new.

156

Her attention was once more diverted back to Queen Shulamit when she noticed the queen was holding something up in her hand. They were silver and rectangular, and they looked—singed? "Esther, do you recognize these?"

Esther shook her head. "No."

"They're hinges," said Queen Shulamit. "I think they're from your violin case."

"From my—where were they?"

Shulamit looked at her uneasily. "In the ashes of the kitchen fire at the inn."

Esther felt like the inside of her skull was a mass of wadded-up laundry. No thoughts would form. She would not let them. "What do you mean?"

"I was looking at this case all wrong," said Queen Shulamit. "I thought our thief was someone who wanted the violin for what it was—either for its monetary value, or for its intrinsic worth. Not someone who wanted it for what its *absence* would be."

"What do you mean, *was*?" said Esther. She put down her plate and felt sweat running down her torso, inside her dress.

"That's how I know it wasn't the innkeeper. He wouldn't have done that. He wouldn't have—" Shulamit looked at her uneasily. "—burnt it."

"No." Esther's trembling fingertips flew to her lips.

"Isaac, please tell everybody what you found last night."

The princess had quieted down some, so Isaac was able to speak relatively uninterrupted. "Last night I went out in my lizard form. I located the residue of sparkling paint in both orange and yellow where it had scraped off on the underside of the bed in Eli's room."

157

Esther whipped her head around to face Eli. "When did you have my case?"

"It was Eli who took your violin," said Queen Shulamit. "I'm sorry. When he was at the marketplace buying your scarf, he overheard someone talking about a shapeshifting potion and took advantage of the opportunity."

"I never did anything like that!" Eli protested. "Esther, tell her!"

To the queen, she protested, "Why would you—" But Esther stopped, thinking about the paint on the bed.

"I didn't have time to do anything like that!" shouted Eli. "I was never gone for that long from the room where we were all eating!"

"You didn't burn it at first. That's why you stuck it under the bed," said Shulamit. "You burned it later."

"The wizard! He's against me!" Eli pointed at Isaac accusingly. "He's lying about the paint on the bed."

Isaac stepped forward and fixed Eli in his piercing blue stare. "You were just going to take it for a few hours, to see how she'd react, to show her a world where she didn't need it. And then, you saw how well she got along with Tzuriel, and you decided she needed to be tied to you more permanently. Into the fire it went."

Eli glared at him, then turned to Shulamit. "You call yourself a fair ruler, but you let this sorcerer break the laws you promised your father you'd uphold? You promised us when you invited a wizard into the palace that he wouldn't be going around reading all our minds."

"He's not," said Shulamit, stony-faced. "He doesn't. But it's awfully interesting that you immediately assumed he was."

158

Chapter 20: Truth and Rebirth

Rivka was tense and ready; at any minute the accused man could lash out either verbally or physically, and if he did, she was in charge of the guards who would subdue him.

Eli looked around him at the roomful of shocked people, then turned toward Esther. "It's for your own good," he said. "It's not healthy for anyone to care about a thing more than they care about the human beings in their life."

"But that's not..." Esther's voice was broken and the tears had started. "You know how important my family—my baby sisters—"

"Your Majesty, you don't understand." Eli turned to face the queen. "She wasn't eating. I mean, I know she's not going to waste away, but think how it made me feel to see her destroying herself over something like this. Isn't that proof that she needed to be jolted out of it?"

"Think how it made *you* feel?" asked Shulamit dryly. Rivka could see the remnants of her interrupted night in her unimpressed face. "You destroyed something not only precious to this woman you're supposed to be in love with, but precious to this throne for historical reasons, and we're supposed to think how it made *you* feel?"

"That thing was ruining my life!"

With one eye on Eli, Rivka glanced quickly at movement she had perceived elsewhere in the room. Micah was looking at her nervously, and she wondered what was going through his mind.

"She was like an addict," Eli continued. "If she was ruining her life from drinking or poppies, you wouldn't question my rescue. She should have been home with her family, with me, starting our life, finally. I've worked for years to study the law, but I can't be

159

an advocate if I'm following her around all the time. Everything was on hold."

"But you said you wanted to come—it wasn't even my idea—" Esther could only weep. Liora walked over and folded her into her arms, and the young woman sobbed on her shoulder.

"Of course I had to come! What would happen if I let you run around the world by yourself?" Eli gestured to Tzuriel. "Think of all the men who would have tried to take advantage of how innocent you are!"

Rivka kept watching Micah, until he finally hopped off his cushion and approached her. "Captain Riv, I've got to talk to you."

Tuning out the rest of Eli's ridiculous defense, she looked at him sharply. "Is it about this? Otherwise, we will talk later."

"It's about this."

"I'm tired of listening to this," called out Shulamit. "Eli, you're under arrest for illegal use of shapeshifting potion, and for theft, and for destruction of a historical treasure."

"You don't understand!" Eli protested as Tivon and another guard took him by both arms.

"You're right!" said Shulamit sharply. "I don't. I understand the kind of love where you support someone's dreams and admire her achievements. *You* are just a selfish manipulator. Don't listen to him, Esther."

Esther peeled the blue scarf off her neck and let it fall to the ground.

"That scarf—that's so you could prompt her to go back to her room for it in the middle of dinner," said Shulamit. "So when the people in the courtyard said they saw her enter her room, she'd have had a reason to go back for real."

160

"And then you tried to blame it on me!" Tzuriel glared at him.

"You were trying to steal her!" Eli snarled.

"You can't steal a human being," bellowed Shulamit. "Guards, seriously, get him out of here. This is *toxic*." Tivon and the other guard hustled him away. Rivka could hear him still protesting as they drifted into the distance.

Meanwhile, Micah whispered to Rivka, "Did you use the ripening crystal or does the wizard still have it?"

"What?" Rivka followed his line of reasoning. "No, I don't want to use it."

"So he has it?"

"I suppose so."

"Will he give it to me if I give you something?"

"I don't know. What are you offering?"

"My violin," said Micah, "because I think it's Esther's."

Rivka looked him deep in the eye. "What do you mean?"

"I didn't know it was hers. I took it from Eli's room. I took it out of the case while he was at dinner. If he threw something on the kitchen fire, it was an empty case."

Rivka exhaled sharply. "Of course we need it back."

"You'll never find it without my help."

"Are you so sure about that?"

"I'm smaller than you are. I can fit in tiny places."

"I don't like to be blackmailed."

161

"I'm not blackmailing. I'm just asking for a deal. What would you do in my place?"

Rivka considered his words. She didn't understand how the magic worked, and, inevitably, it would be up to Isaac. But thanks to Micah's street morality, he had the potential to restore Esther's happiness. "Go be a man, instead of a boy, and ask him yourself. I think he'll say yes."

She watched him scamper across the room to where her husband stood holding the infant princess and plead his case. An expression she didn't understand came into Isaac's face for a moment, his eyes moving from side to side slowly. Then he smiled gently, and Micah's body language became triumphant.

He faced the others. "Esther—"

"Hmm?" The young woman turned her tearstained face from Liora's shoulder at the sound of her name.

"Your violin is safe. I stole it from Eli the same night he took it from you, before he burned the case."

"What?" She scrambled to her feet. "You mean it?"

"I thought it was his," Micah explained. "I didn't like him because he laughed at me when I was begging for food. I missed my violin from back home, so I figured I'd paid for it with my dignity. Or something." He shrugged. "Anyway, you can have it back now."

"Riv, go with him," Shulamit commanded.

"Of course."

"I didn't know you played," said Esther. She took his hands in hers. "Are you any good?"

"We played together the other night—I thought he did well," said Rivka. "Come on, Micah."

162

♫

Aviva sat in the kitchen-house, grinding chickpeas into meal for falafels. Her shoulders swayed to the lively melody that floated in from some other part of the palace, and she felt a deep, sweet peace inside at the idea that Esther and her precious violin had been reunited. For it must be her—she recognized the melody from the recital, and besides, she had every confidence in the brain of her beloved Queen Shulamit.

She smiled broadly to welcome the queen into the room. "So the songbird is reborn?"

"Yes, but at a cost."

Aviva looked at her meaningfully. "You mean Eli?"

"That's got to be rough." Shulamit collapsed into one of the chairs. "I'm letting her stay in the palace overnight to recuperate."

"What about your other mystery?"

"Oh, the clasp design?" Shulamit hid a yawn, not very well. "Gershom had to go to jail, unfortunately, because of the potion he used. He won't be there long, but hopefully he'll learn his lesson. And Zev said that it was all right for him to use the clasp design once he got out as long as he gave him credit in the shop and paid him rent on it."

"Who's watching his shop in the meantime?"

"One of Dafna's kids." Shulamit snorted. "If they want to go to the Sugar Coast and stay up all night partying, let them earn the fare. Speaking of staying up all night! Our poor little daughter."

"You hustled her away before I could do anything," Aviva pouted.

"No reason for both of us to get no sleep," Shulamit pointed out. "Poor little thing." She caressed Naomi's tiny head.

163

"And we have more sour oranges to look forward to," said Aviva. "This is only one tooth. Soon, she'll summon all her friends!"

"It's what we signed up for." Shulamit looked exhausted but contented.

"Still want more?"

"Yes, but not for a few years!" Shulamit yawned. "And I know you still want to bear one." The yawn persisted. "Ugggh. Now that I don't have to put on my public face for all those people, I can't stop!"

"You should nap, now that all your mysteries are solved."

"I will. I need it."

When Shulamit left, Aviva was by herself again until lunchtime. She noticed with interest that the violin music had split into a duet, and wondered if Liora had gone home to get her own instrument. Or perhaps it was Micah, playing on a borrowed fiddle from Tzuriel. Either way, it made the morning's work seem magical and assisted by fairies.

When Rivka and Isaac arrived for lunch, they had Micah in tow. "Look at this hard worker!" Rivka said proudly. "All morning he carried supplies for the men who were fixing the roof. He was very helpful!"

"Then I'll definitely give you a meal!" Aviva carried the platter of falafels to the table. "Then it wasn't you I heard playing duets with Esther?"

"That was Liora," said Isaac. "She went home to get her violin and spent a few hours keeping Esther company."

"See? I told you they aren't competition." Shulamit was last to enter, the baby princess strapped to her chest.

164

Lunch was over quickly, and Shulamit rose to study some legal documents. The others remained, Rivka relaxing with a mug of mead, and Isaac distracting the clearly nervous Micah with stories of his and Rivka's days in battle together. Aviva stood at a basin on the counter, scrubbing the dishes from lunch to a sparkling clean.

She could feel the atmosphere in the room change when Isaac retrieved the gem from his pocket.

Micah's hands rested on the table, slowly moving the fig-colored crystal around between his fingers. "Will my voice get deeper?"

"I think that is likely, yes," said Isaac.

"Will it make me tall? Will it make me broad?"

"I don't know," said Isaac. "You're tall enough now, but perhaps."

"For broad you can always work your muscles as I do," Rivka pointed out. "There is a technique to it, and I will teach you."

"Will I grow a beard?" Micah looked intently at Isaac's face, at his delicate goatee.

"Perhaps," said Isaac. "I think so."

"Will other things grow?" Micah continued nervously, but with resolution in his tone.

"I don't know," said Isaac. "Maybe that is only for you to know."

Micah looked at the crystal again, then lifted it to his lips. Rivka pushed over her mug, ready to ease its passage, and Micah picked it up in his other hand. "Today, I am a man!"

Rivka chuckled, and Isaac said, "It's never too late to say that."

165

"To the new me," Micah continued quietly, then engulfed the crystal with his mouth. A swig of mead followed, and he swallowed hard.

"To ripening," said Aviva from her dishes, lifting the clean plate in her hand into the air to honor him.

Chapter 21: Hold Your Arm Closed

Isaac left Micah in Rivka's more than capable hands and made his way across the courtyard. On his way, he met Esther. The hair around her face was damp and she looked out of sorts, but she smiled when she saw him. "Isaac, right?"

"Yes, that's me."

"I was washing my face in the creek behind the palace," she explained. "So I could tell myself I was done with crying."

"It doesn't make you feel better to cry, to let it out?"

"I don't know." She looked lost. "I was wondering, could you come and keep me company for a little while? Ever since I saw you holding the baby princess—I thought of my sisters—anyway, if the queen trusts you with her most precious... but maybe you don't have time and this is very inappropriate and I'm just a bother—"

"Come and tell *Zayde* the Wizard your troubles." Isaac looked on her warmly and gestured back toward her room.

"That's *grandfather* where you come from, right?" Esther led him back into the chamber the queen had graciously lent to her. "I didn't get as far away as that on my tour."

"Will you continue, now that you have back your fiddle?"

"Yes, actually—" She sat down on the sofa and tucked a stray lock of hair behind her ear. "Liora and I will be on tour together."

"Ahh, so the duets we all enjoyed this morning—"

"You liked it?"

"First rate!"

"We'll go back to my hometown first. More than anything I want to see my family right now," said Esther. "Oh, and I've asked Micah to come along as my, I don't know, water boy or something. Liora says she raised enough money playing in the park on my behalf that she bought him his own violin, although I'm sure Tzuriel undercharged her, and we'll both be giving him lessons, food, and a place to sleep in exchange for his duties."

"Tzuriel seems like a good man."

Esther inhaled a momentous breath. "Yes, he's already given me a case to replace the one that burned up." She gestured with her foot at the new case, plain but sturdy, sitting at the foot of the bed.

Isaac noticed that her wording avoided blaming Eli for the fate of the original case. "No butterflies," he commented genially, avoiding the topic.

"No, not yet." A smile escaped from the desolation of her face. "He said we could paint it later, but for now it's blank and clean."

"A beautiful idea."

"It is." Esther's expression darkened. "But do I deserve it? I keep flashing back to what Eli said and wondering if I'm doing everything all wrong."

"I remember his lips moved a lot, but nothing of value came out."

"He was hurting so much. He kept saying how I wasn't considering his feelings. How I could never empathize. How my music humiliated him. How it embarrassed and frightened him when I made friends if they were men." Esther cast up her hands in frustration. "I'm sure he'd even be mad if he knew I were in here talking to you—and you've got to be twice my age!"

"More than that," said Isaac, but not without amusement.

"Oh no—I didn't mean—oh, I'm sorry."

168

"I do not want to be young again," Isaac reassured her.

"He said I was keeping him around for convenience..."

"Were you?"

"I don't even know what that means! He said—"

Isaac held up one finger on his left hand to silence her, then slowly revealed the scar that ran across his right palm and down the underbelly of his forearm.

Esther's eyes bugged out, and then she caught herself. "What happened?"

"At one time I was not only a wizard, but a warrior," said Isaac. "I was sliced open in battle and can no longer close this hand." He strained his fingers to demonstrate, noticing Esther wince—most likely at the idea that such an injury would wipe out someone's ability to play violin as she did.

"How long ago did it happen?"

"Before you were born."

Esther's eyes widened. "So your whole life, pretty much."

Her self-centered innocence made him smile. "I want to tell you about it, because there is a lesson there for how you should go forth from today. You, too, have been sliced open."

"Yes..." She understood.

Isaac often told of the scar's history, to entertain new guards in training, or to enthrall the children of visiting foreign royalty. But while he usually talked about the adventure that led to it, of the rescue of the kidnapped boy prince and the capture of the pretender, of the plot and how the wizards had uncovered it, today was different. Today...

"Not everyone who seeks magical training finishes the study," Isaac began. "During my acolyte years, there was a man who didn't finish. I met him later on the battlefield, once I became a full wizard, during a mission with my order."

"Did he have any powers?"

"No, I don't think so," said Isaac. "He never got as far as that. He knew me, but we were fighting on different sides, and he was just as devoted to his side as I was to mine. With swords we faced each other, but I was too secure in my own abilities and tried to use magic and swordplay at the same time. As I lifted my left hand to send a bolt of energy in his direction, he gashed upward, at my right hand where I held my sword."

"Ouch." Esther winced.

"Naturally, I lost the sword," Isaac continued. "In that split second, then, I had to make a decision. Humiliated and angry, I longed to continue the battle, to take up the sword with my left hand, or to use the magic I had been about to aim his way. But this part of the arm..." He ran his left pointer finger up and down his scar. "If it opens, the blood comes out too quickly and death is very fast."

"So what did you do?"

"I chose life. I chose... humiliation, but I chose to keep myself alive. With every ounce of magic in my body, I concentrated on holding the wound in my arm closed and ran for safety. There were other wizards, you see, to take my place anyway. It did not hurt the fight."

"Did anyone help you?"

"Nobody saw what happened. I disappeared into the forest and took my snake form—I thought, well, a snake has no arms, so maybe nothing will hurt. I was wrong. My whole body burned. It was as if the gash traveled the length of my whole body."

"How horrible!"

"Again and again the thoughts assaulted me, *You could have stayed to fight! How dare he! He, whose skill was less than mine. He, who had failed to complete magical training.* All these arguments."

"But you would have died."

"Exactly. And that's why I had to keep reminding myself that I held my arm closed, that in order to live it was vital that I hold my arm closed. I could not do both. Each time I felt the old anger, I thought of my arm. It shows me I made the right choice."

"Are you trying to tell me that in order to heal, I have to stop arguing with Eli in my mind?"

"Already you understand." Isaac patted her hand. "Just think of me each time one of his pieces of nonsense rises up in your mind. Don't argue with it—simply dismiss it. For if you argue, you will find yourself arguing again, forever. He was wrong, but you fear him anyway. Hold your arm closed. Let him continue being wrong, far from your heart."

"Far from my heart," she echoed dully.

"Hold your arm closed."

"Yes." She turned toward him. "It's an amazing story. I'm sorry it never healed properly, though."

"That may happen with you as well, but it doesn't keep me from living my life," he explained. "I learned to write and wield a sword with my left hand; magic helps with plenty of other things. The scar you may bear from Eli will hold nothing to the magic you'll discover as you open up to all the new things he prevented you from experiencing."

"Hold my arm closed," she murmured. "So the magic wouldn't help it heal right?"

"No," he said. "I bound my hand myself, since it would be a while since I could get to anyone with medical training. I bound it tightly and with my fingers outstretched, so I could still aim magic through my fingertips."

"So you can still do magic on that side?"

"Of course!"

"Hold my arm closed," Esther repeated. "What happened to the other man? Do you know?"

Isaac's mind flashed over a series of images—years later, helping his former opponent under completely unrelated circumstances, perhaps even saving his life. It made him feel selfishly powerful to be in that position, and for some reason his pride had kept him from revealing the permanent nature and depth of the injury. Well.

"That isn't important for you right now," was what he said out loud. "Look to your own future. Keep yourself safe. Concentrate on your music—and on your new friends."

"Liora's got such a deep heart when you get to know her," said Esther. "Eli kept saying she—Oh, right." She grinned self-consciously.

"See? You can do it."

He left her late in the afternoon, returning to her fiddle with renewed dedication to her art, to God, and to herself. It was time to clear his head—he didn't regret the way he'd comforted her for a moment, but kicking up all the dust around his long-ago adventure had taken a lot out of him emotionally. Esther had washed away her tears in the creek. Maybe a trip out back would be good for him too. His throat felt dry, too, from all that talking.

Rivka was there ahead of him, scrubbing her feet in the cool, sparkling water.

Isaac, as usual, felt as happy to see her as if they hadn't met in weeks. "I wanted a drink, but I also found something tasty!"

"You know it," Rivka shot back.

"I'm exhausted, Mighty One."

"*You're* exhausted?" She raised an eyebrow. "I just taught Micah every bodybuilding exercise I know. He's a sweet boychik. Would have let me use the crystal myself—he thinks I'm like him, of course. I wonder what would happen if I had. Not become a man."

"I bet your mask would disappear," said Isaac evenly.

To his surprise, Rivka's eyes looked thoughtful and welcoming rather than the shuttered windows this topic usually conjured. "Someday..."

He fixed her with a heartfelt stare. "If you decide to unmask, you know I'm with you every step of the way."

"If I unmask... it can't be just about me," said Rivka. "Even if I'm wrong that my reputation would be dismissed as impossible, as lies—then I become exceptional. I become 'Rivka the Mighty,' not proof that women can be soldiers."

"So what are you thinking?"

"I think I will recruit a group of young women for a women's unit to join the queen's royal guard," said Rivka. "Do you remember that girl in the City of Red Clay who practically wanted to run away with us? Maybe we can find her again. There will be so many more like her too. And if I unmask, it will be after we *all* prove, together, that women can fight."

"I like this," said Isaac, amazed, "and I will help however you need me to."

"I never doubted you would," was Rivka's response.

"Dafna knows I took the transformation stone," said Isaac, "and people talk. It's possible many of them will think I used it to help my male lover become a woman."

Rivka shrugged. "People are already making up stories about me. Not much I can do about it, so I don't care—as long as they believe the truth about my abilities."

"Shulamit will need to be more emphatically open about her inclinations," Isaac pointed out. "Without us standing there as brawny reminders to respect same-sex pairings, she'll need to be the public face of it herself."

"She's never hid it—people are just..." Rivka waved her hand dismissively. "Well, she'll be fine. She's ready. It already frustrates her how easily people are willing to ignore what's right in front of them if it doesn't fit the ideas they already had. So where were you all afternoon?"

"Comforting Esther."

"Oh." Rivka snorted. "That Eli was a piece of work. What does he know from love? He loves himself, that one."

"When someone loves a remarkable woman..." Isaac sat down on her right side and caressed the firm line of her biceps with his left hand. It stirred his blood. "...her feats should captivate him, just as her eyes do."

"Do you catalogue my feats, then?"

"Each," he replied. "Back to that first moment I knew I loved you, the first time you beat me during our sword fighting lessons."

"It was raining," she remembered.

"You stood there, hair wet, water dripping everywhere, staring at me, confused and triumphant... You were an avalanche."

After five years they had grown used to kissing with the cloth mask in the way. He smelled the sweat of her busy afternoon on it.

"I remember those old days..." His fingers were in her hair now. "I, bored and frustrated in the countryside, and you, proud and eager, but rough around the edges..."

"I love you because you never tried to smooth me out."

"No," said Isaac. "I *sharpened* you."

Chapter 22: Ripe in the Fullness of Harvest

"Vimaaaa! Vima!"

"Vima's right here; she's just looking at the celery," said Shulamit to the tiny child, who was now old enough to walk, as long as her hand was firmly inside of at least one of her mothers'. "See that man? He's selling vegetables. Celery, parsley, carrots, cilantro..."

"Vima."

"Yes, she's right there." This happened all the time. She couldn't figure it out—sometimes it would be her own week, sometimes Aviva's week—Naomi seemed to switch back and forth at random. She was happiest, of course, when she could see both of them.

"I'm here, baby girl!" Aviva turned around, the bag on her shoulder now full of celery and parsley. She bent down to nuzzle the princess's nose. "I just had to get vegetables. You like your vegetables!"

"Veh."

Aviva took Naomi's other hand, and the two women walked the painstakingly slow but blessed walk of toddler parents.

"Hard to imagine she'll be queen someday," Shulamit murmured. "Especially when she drools like that."

"You drool when you fall asleep in my lap," said Aviva.

Shulamit stuck out her tongue.

"Your Majesty!"

Whipping her head around, a smile spread across her face as she spotted Esther of the Singing Hands waving from the entrance of a nearby shop. "Esther! You've come back."

"Yes, but only for a little while. I wanted to see Liora, to thank her for everything she did for me last year, and we were passing through anyway."

"Aaaa!" said Naomi.

Esther bent down to address her directly. "Why, your Highness, you've grown so much! My goodness!"

"Naomi, do you remember Esther? She's the one who makes those pretty noises," said Shulamit. "Remember when she stayed in our palace?"

"I think you have a lovely name, Naomi," said Esther. "Can you say 'Esther'?"

"Ima Vima," was her response.

"Vima?" asked Esther.

"It's what she calls me," Aviva explained.

"The original plan was for me to be Ima and for Aviva to go by *Mammeh*, which is Ima in their language." Shulamit gestured behind her at the ever-present Rivka and Isaac. "But she's a smart little thing, and she must have picked up on the 'viva' part of Aviva. So now she's Vima."

"Like a bima in a temple," said Esther. "How funny!"

"I can accept Aviva as a temple," Shulamit joked flirtatiously.

"Esther!" called a deep, youthful voice from inside the shop. "What about this one?"

177

"Micah, you already bought her that hair ribbon in Ir Ilan, and you made that little woven bracelet," Esther admonished him. "You need to save *some* of your pocket money for rosin and strings or you'll wind up short again like that time Liora had to bail you out." She smiled self-consciously at the queen. "I'm sorry, he and one of my baby sisters are special to each other. He writes to her constantly."

"No need to apologize," said Shulamit. "That's part of the responsibility! I'm sure Aviva and I will have the same kind of conversation with this one in another dozen years. You're doing a great job with him, by the way."

"Thank you so much," said Esther. "I have to tell you— sometimes it's intimidating... and I'm so young myself. But I'm not doing it alone. I have Tzuriel's full support."

Shulamit's eyes twinkled. "I was hoping his name would come up. So he's still around?"

"Yes, he's actually around here somewhere buying supplies." Esther looked around. "He's not here to sell anything this time. We're just passing through." Micah emerged from the shop, and she put her arm around him, which he accepted for two seconds before untangling himself.

"Have you seen much of each other?"

"Yes, he joined up with Liora and I when our tour reached the Sugar Coast," said Esther, "and then, when the tour was over, Micah and I took him back home with us. He set up shop in Lovely Valley and got to know my family. So did Micah. It was such a balm, I can't tell you, after what I'd been through..." She took the queen's hands in hers. "Thank you—for setting me free."

"Of course," said Shulamit, bowing her head slightly in acceptance of the honor. She looked deeply into Esther's eyes. "You're a daughter of my realm, and even though I'm just a few years older than you are, that makes you my daughter too. Your welfare was entrusted to me by the memory of my father. I'm only grateful I was able to help you. It's the best part of the job."

"Really? Not the new clothes and the roomful of books?" Aviva teased, the infant princess hefted up now onto her ample hip.

Shulamit raised an eyebrow. "Better than every purple dress in the kingdom."

"You still didn't say anything about the books."

Shulamit made a grotesque face, and it had its intended effect. Both Aviva and the baby burst into peals of laughter.

"You two are so cute!" Esther exclaimed. "Oh, I'm sorry. Was that inappropriate?"

"Don't be so afraid," Rivka interjected. "You're not a bother, you've never been a bother, you're not inappropriate, and you're a very lovely woman."

Esther chuckled. "You sound like Tzuriel."

"He's right," Rivka said. "So, *nu*, tell us! Shulamit is of course trying to be delicate, but there is nothing delicate about Riv Maror. When's the wedding?"

Esther burst out laughing. "We'll be married in the Sugar Coast—maybe even on the beach!—but I guess that'll be up to all his aunties, and then we'll be back on the road." She was beaming. "Up north this time, back through Imbrio and Zembluss and probably even as far as where you two come from."

"You must be so excited, Micah," said the queen warmly.

"Sure!" he said enthusiastically. "The only thing I'm worried about is how I don't speak any of those languages up there. I mean, Tzuriel knows plenty of languages, but then I just stand around looking clueless."

179

"Well, don't forget that if they worship as we do, their prayers will be in our language," Shulamit reminded him. "So they've got to know at least a little bit."

"Sure, if I want to bless stuff. But what if I want to tell them I'm thirsty?"

"*Ikh bin dorshtik,*" said Isaac.

"You'll do fine," Rivka reassured him. "The best way to learn a language is to live in the place where they speak it every day. When I was traveling the lands as a mercenary warrior, with Isaac trapped in his dragon form by a curse so I didn't know he had survived the attack on my home, I worked in plenty of places with unfamiliar tongues. Each time I had to pick up a new language, I practiced it night after night, sleeping outside in the wilderness with my dragon for a pillow." She chuckled. "In fact, I told him about himself. I'd practice my new skills, by telling the creature I thought was just my steed all about my dead lover. *Oy vey*, was I silly! With him right there curled up around me listening the whole time."

"It made for nice bedtime stories," said Isaac modestly.

"Can I see your dragon form?" Micah asked excitedly. "I've never seen a dragon up close."

"I'll do better than that." Isaac bent down from his immense height and fixed Micah with a dramatic stare. "I'll take you up in the air if you want—you and Esther."

Esther and Micah looked at each other, open-mouthed and wide-eyed. "Oh, wow, that would be amazing!" he exclaimed.

"What a wonderful thing to offer!" said Esther. "Yes, please." She grinned nervously.

"Let's get out of the market so I have room to transform." Isaac began walking. "And so we don't cause a riot."

While they walked, Shulamit slithered back around to where she could talk to Esther again, personally. "Esther, thank you for saying I set you free. But in some ways, you've done a lot of the hard work yourself, and I wanted to give you credit for that."

"Thank you, Your Majesty." Esther looked thoughtful. "Micah calls that thing he swallowed a ripening crystal."

"That was Aviva's nickname for it, yes. I love the way she talks."

"He's ripened nicely... I guess, in a way, I've ripened too."

"It's sweet to be ripe," Aviva piped up from behind them.

They stopped on the edge of a wide grassland. "Watch this," Isaac said dramatically, and before their eyes, his black-green dragon form arose. Antelopes that had been grazing at the edge of the field scattered as he flapped his wings once, sending Esther's and Rivka's hair whirling.

"Amazing!" Micah shouted.

"He's all mine," said Rivka with a smirk, mostly to herself.

"Climb on board," said the dragon.

Rivka and Micah helped Esther climb onto his back, and when she was comfortable, Rivka lifted Micah up to sit in front of her. "Have you got me?" he asked Esther, craning his head around slightly.

"I've got you," she responded.

Off into the air they flew, with Rivka left behind on the ground to guard the two mothers and their baby. She put an arm around each of their shoulders. "See how happy they are, *Malkeleh*? You did that."

181

"Not really," Shulamit repeated. "They did a lot of that themselves."

She rested her head on Aviva's shoulder, kissed Naomi, and was content.

END

♫

Thank you's and standing ovations to:

To Virginia Lamboley, who found true love when her viola was stolen, and knows how to tell a good story

To Kate Thomas O'Gara, who I've already thanked in the dedication, but deserves another one for working so hard on cleaning this up, and to Rania, for her own careful scrutiny

To the rest of my orchestra cohorts, including Margaret and especially Masatoshi, who helped with some of the editing since I was doing it between rehearsals and who lent me a kalimba and a steel drum so that I wasn't flying in the dark

To my spouse, "When someone loves a remarkable woman, her feats should captivate her, just as her eyes do."

To my mother, for putting a fiddle in my hand when I was four, and to my stepfather, for putting chords under my melodies.

To Mei-mei Luo, Dr. Janna Lower, Ralph Blizard, Marty Spencer, and everyone else who guided my bow in childhood and adolescence

To the brave women who helped me with details I am lucky enough not to have personal experience to know

To Caitlin, Nikki, Tof, Karen, Breianna, and Mycroft, for additional help, and to Kofi, for insisting that I put The Islands in my books somehow.

To Ducky, Jane, and Kat, my test audience

To Becca and all my other artists

To the Jumblr kids, your support means the world to me. I wish you all the best of luck in life.

To Chef Anthony, whose juice booth is not to be missed at my local farmer's market. So good I had to put it in a book!

To Jacques Offenbach, James Morris, Susan Quittmeyer Morris, Roberta Alexander, Hans-Peter König, Anna Netrebko, Wolfgang Amadeus Mozart, and, well, René Pape (again!) for truly moving inspiration

To the folks at Prizm, especially Kristi, Jaymi, Amanda, and Jo, for helping to get this show on the road! Shows move on but they remember every hall they've played.

Glossary of non-English words in *A Harvest of Ripe Figs*

Some of them seem like English to me, because they were a constant part of my upbringing and remain a constant in my life! But, I realize that many Gentile (non-Jewish) readers would like more information about some of those words, and likewise that not all Jewish readers share my background. It was my hope that I had incorporated them organically, so that they could be understood in context the way one would understand invented words in any other fantasy novel. But why not give people the opportunity to learn more?

The conceit of the Mangoverse is that Perach, the setting, is a Hebrew-speaking haven of tropical agriculture, and that up north, several countries away, there's a country whose primary language is Yiddish. "Perach" itself means "flower" in Hebrew, and is a reference to Perach's being based on South Florida, where I grew up. (Florida also means "flower", in a way.)

What follows is an informal glossary, maybe a little out of order. I don't claim to be an expert in Judaica, but I'd like to offer what I have.

Aba – Dad in Hebrew (Mom is **Ima**.) Incidentally **Mammeh** is Yiddish for "Mom". (Dad is "**Tateh**", and they're both the same words in Polish, which makes sense — Yiddish is in a lot of ways Polish-flavored German written in Hebrew letters.)

Malka – Queen (with Malkeleh meaning "little queen", commonly used for a little girl in one's life, even if she's not royalty–the way my dad used to call my little half-sister "Princess." Rivka's use of **Malkeleh** as a pet name for the queen is therefore a pun.)

By the way, the -eleh ending for a name to make a diminutive is a Yiddishism. Hence "**Avivaleh**" at one point, for Aviva.

Zayde—Grandpa in Yiddish. Grandma is **Bubby** (often spelled **Bubbe**.)

Maror – horseradish. Well, "bitter herbs", anyway.

Ir Ilan means Oak Town in Hebrew.

Schmendrick – another one of those undefinable Yiddish insults

Sherwani—NOT a Hebrew or Yiddish word; this is an Indian men's long dress coat.

Shabbat (or **Shabbos**, in Yiddish — Shabbat is Hebrew) is Friday night and Saturday morning. The Jewish Sabbath, involving compulsory rest, special food, candle-lighting, going to **shul** (Yiddish word for temple/synagogue which is the same as the German word for school), and supposedly, marital sex

Chazzer—pig in Yiddish

Shamash—On Chanukah, the way you light the menorah is that you light the candle in the center first, and then use that candle to light the other candles. That center candle is the shamash.

Oy—literally "Oh" in Yiddish but it means *so much more than that.* Also, my grandmother always pronounced it "Uy", but I have no idea how much of that was Brooklyn or what.

Ikh bin dorshtik—"I am thirsty" in Yiddish. Interesting to compare it to German, where they don't say "I am thirsty", they literally say "I have thirst" (*Ich habe durst.*) I have similar fun comparing the word for onion – Tzibbeleh vs. Zweibel. (The German "z" has the same sound as the Hebrew, and therefore Yiddish, letter that does the "tz" thing like in Tzuriel's name. Just like in *Mozart.*)

Bima—the elevated front part of the temple Where Stuff Happens.

Boureka—Many cultures have a savory "pastry pocket with stuff in it"; this is ours.

Boychik—affectionate way to talk to a boy, equivalent to the English slang "little man."

Schmegeggeh—Yiddish is full of colorful insults that are hard to define. (The accented syllable is the middle one.)

Tales from Outer Lands
by Shira Glassman

In memory of Shippo the Lizard, 2004-2014

Rivka in Port Saltspray

With grateful thanks to Nicole, Dr. Caroti, Leigh Alanna, and my mother for their assistance.

The dark man with the earring shook his head. "I don't care how big of a sword you're carrying; I'm not letting horses on my ship." He folded his arms across his chest and leaned back against one of the posts on the dock. Behind him, seagulls swooped through the air in both directions over his vessel as it lay anchored in the water.

Rivka, who went by Riv and was posing as a man, mostly so that conversations like this weren't even worse than they already were, blurted out, "But what if--?"

"Look, what's the big deal? Both armies have plenty of money behind them -- whichever side you decide to fight on, they'll give you a horse. Probably a better one than you've got now." The man was looking her up and down, probably judging her based on her tattered pants and scuffed boots. It had been a thin month. This port town had plenty of police of its own and didn't need a mercenary -- one of the reasons she was trying to get to Zembluss as soon as possible, to see if their civil war couldn't solve her money problems.

"No, it won't," Rivka barked impatiently. "Mine turns into a dragon."

"It what?"

189

"She turns into a dragon."

"I am not letting a *dragon* on my ship! What's wrong with you? The other soldiers would never--"

"What if she flies next to the boat as a dragon and then comes back as a horse from time to time to rest?" Rivka, who didn't often panic, was beginning to run out of options. "That way you wouldn't have a horse--"

"*Ship.*"

"What?"

"It's not a boat, it's a ship."

Rivka sighed and consciously prevented herself from kicking the man in the groin, because it would have solved nothing. "What if she flew next to the *ship*--"

"Why can't she just fly you over the sea the whole way?" The man swatted at a nearby seagull who had decided to alight on the railing and beg for snacks.

"I--" Rivka didn't quite know how to explain the dragon's mysterious lack of stability. Sometimes her dragon powers just ebbed away without warning. Over the open ocean, that might prove lethal. Unless she also turned out to have surprise dolphin powers. The dragon form had initially been a surprise, so Rivka supposed she might have other hidden forms that hadn't manifested yet.

"Look, I'm sorry, son," said the man. "I can see how badly you want this. But I think your best option is to wait for another ship."

But I need the signing bonus tonight, Rivka didn't say. *The innkeeper is cheating me and has my horse held hostage in his barn until I pay him for charges he invented. And your port town is corrupt, so the police won't do anything, especially since they see me as competition.*

What she did tell him was, in her own language, to shit in the sea. And then she couldn't help but laugh bitterly, behind the cloth mask that hid the lower half of her face, because there it was, the sea -- right there. Ready for him.

But not for her, apparently. Or her horse. Dragon. Something.

Rivka paced the streets of Port Saltspray, only half seeing the shops and people she passed. She had no incentive to hurry back to the inn, instead using the time to rack her brains for ideas for quick cash. What else could she sell? Not her sword. Not only was it her livelihood, but it was one of her only two mementos of the dead man whose love still warmed her heart. Isaac was the first person to see the warrior within her, and he had taught her everything he knew about combat. The wizard had been dead a year and a half, but she still dreamed of him at night. When she woke up clutching the charred fragment of his robes that had survived the fire that claimed him, she was able to steady herself again by taking up the sword he had given her.

So, selling it was not an option. But neither was giving up Dragon. The horse-dragon-something was her family now, since she'd run away from her mother and uncle and taken to life on the road. She walked past the butcher shop, and it reminded her of the times she and Dragon had happily hunted wild deer together, sharing their catch. Now past the blacksmith, and she smelled iron and thought of battle, and felt the horse's muscles beneath hers. They moved together like a joint beast, reading each other's intentions. A woman was selling pillows on the street, and Rivka thought about how often she had slept outside in the middle of nowhere, curled up against the sleeping dragon. She probably bored her silly with endless bedtime stories about Isaac, but she was also pretty sure she was just a beast who couldn't understand spoken language beyond the ordinary commands that any trained animal did. So Rivka didn't see any reason to discontinue the practice, especially since it helped her keep Isaac with her.

She didn't have much, then -- a dead man, a live beast, and steel.

What about prize money? Sometimes there were combat competitions, and at five feet eleven inches, with muscles that bore witness to years of training, and stamina and a body type inherited from the laborer father she'd never known, she knew they were a good option.

♡ ✿ ♡

"Hey!"

She'd gotten back to the inn and was addressing the room.

Men looked up from their beers suspiciously, some reaching for their weapons. "No, I'm not a threat," she added. "Is there any prizefighting in Port Saltspray?"

The men all looked at each other. Some shrugged. Some looked away.

Rivka got the distinct feeling they had all decided to keep information from unwelcome outsiders. With her wild mane of blonde hair flowing past her shoulders and her guttural accent, she knew she stood out even if plenty of the other men in the room had muscles to rival hers.

She slammed her butt into a seat in the corner and rested her chin on her hand, staring into space. Maybe it was for the best. With warriors flooding into Port Saltspray from all over the country headed for the boats -- ships -- bound for Zembluss and its civil war, not to mention refugees from Zembluss itself, winning might not have been as much of a guarantee as she'd initially thought.

A mug of beer slid in her direction across the table, appearing as if by magic and unbidden. Dismissing the ridiculous fantasy that Isaac had somehow awoken from the dead (and found her hundreds of miles away from home, then used his wizard tricks to move beer steins around), she growled, "I can't pay for that," as she turned around.

It wasn't Isaac -- obviously. Instead, it was a young man with his hair in a braid and a stuffy, buttoned-up dress coat that looked two sizes too big for him. Frilly lace poured out of his collar, and Rivka noticed there were even ruffles coming out from under his cuffs. His gaze was darting around the room as if he were afraid to be around so many toughs, and indeed, he could hardly have looked more out of place.

"Excuse me, sir, but are you a warrior looking for work?" He spoke timidly but with an elegant tone.

Scholar? Young nobleman? Rivka tried to place him. Obviously, he was here out of his element, and she guessed he'd only come here looking for someone like her. "Why? Who are you?"

"The name's Waterweed. I heard you asking about prizefighting, and... and I need someone to rescue my fiancée."

Rivka's eyebrows lifted. Work? Real work? "What's happened?"

"She's being held by the people of the mountain," explained the young man. "They've promised her hand in marriage to the winner of a... friendly combat." His face contorted with pain as he spoke. "You have to believe me that I'd go and fight for her, even though I don't know what I'm doing -- if only I could."

With his right hand, he gestured to his left arm. It hung limply by his side.

"Your arm?" Rivka asked, wiping away sweat that had suddenly formed under her cloth mask. Heat flooded her face, and she thought of Isaac's permanently injured right hand.

"Accident with a horse," he said shyly, looking down at the table. "Anyway, I'd be the first to be eliminated. But I love her, and she loves me. I swore I'd do anything I could to save her, and if I don't have a left arm, what I do have is money to hire one. You look like you could be twenty arms. What does a left arm cost?"

Rivka did some math in her head, doubling the innkeeper's ransom on her horse, just in case, and adding a bribe for the next ship captain so she could be sure of getting both her *and* her horse across the sea to Zembluss. She announced a figure.

"I'll give you that, and more. Just get her back, safe and sound."

"When is the contest?" Rivka hoped she didn't sound too desperate.

"Tomorrow, after midday."

"And how far away is it?"

"Just outside the city, up in the hills," said Waterweed. "I can draw you a map."

"Can't you come with me? She'd probably feel safer if she saw you there."

Waterweed looked down at the table. "I'd be a liability, really... they'd probably capture me for ransom as soon as they saw me. I'm truly useless in a fight."

"Rough crowd, then?"

He nodded and motioned for the barwoman to come over. "Dinner for two, please?"

Rivka was glad to be fed and seized meat and bread by the handful when the barwoman returned. "Why won't the police help you?"

Her new client snickered amiably. "You're new here, aren't you? They're outside the city limits, so it doesn't exist to them."

Rivka snorted. "Someone should clean this place up."

Waterweed smiled dreamily. "Maybe someday I will. With my wife by my side."

Rivka approached the stable, hoping the innkeeper's grooms weren't in as much of a mood for a fight as she was. They looked more alert than she would have liked. "Relax -- I'm just visiting," she muttered, hands out, but they were tense hands. Anyone could have seen that, and she didn't care who did. Let them know that she was cranky.

Some of the edge went away when she saw Dragon, standing peacefully in one of the stalls. "Hey, girl! *Shayna maydeleh*, pretty girl. They better be treating you good." Rivka patted her gently.

The horse couldn't reply, of course, but her big brown eyes looked healthy and she didn't seem agitated. Even allowing for the fact that she was likely soothed by Rivka's presence, her ears relaxed and her head down, her mood didn't seem to indicate any recent mistreatment.

Still, she was trapped, and that meant Rivka was trapped -- which the warrior hated. Any warrior would.

In her own language, Rivka told the horse all about the fancy young man at the inn. "I have to go on an adventure without you -- sorry you'll have to miss all the fun!" It would have been awfully convenient to just ride in on a dragon and swoop the poor woman away to safety. But Rivka also figured that in a place as screwed up as Port Saltspray, any such "illegal" attempt to interfere with what was going on might draw ire from the police. If she won the woman fair and square -- ugh, what a disgusting concept, "winning" a human being as a prize -- then nobody would be able to question her or even arrest her.

"It's a good thing he came along too," she mused as she ran her hand lightly down the horse's nose. "I would have had to hire myself out as day labor, and by the time I earned enough to get to Zembluss, the war would be over!" She thought about her unknown father, the brawny farmhand who had gotten her mother

195

pregnant as a teenager before being run off the estate by her uncle. He'd never been much in her thoughts, her uncle having filled that void even if badly, but now that sharing his life's work loomed over her, he seemed more real than usual.

The horse named Dragon closed her eyes and leaned her big, soft head against Rivka's chest, tranquil and trusting. Rivka gave her fur gentle scritches as she spoke. "I hope they're feeding you enough. That man in there, Mr. Waterweed, or something, he fed me up good. I made sure he did that, and saved some for the morning, too, so my muscles work like they should."

She eyed the stall and was relieved to see straw, mash, and even half of an apple. Then she remembered that if the innkeeper wound up keeping Dragon, he would most likely sell her -- leaving him every incentive not to starve the poor creature -- and her stomach grew heavy again. "He was such a funny sight, Dragon, that man," she continued, changing the subject as much to soothe herself as to commune with her horse. "One of his eyes was blue, but the other was brown! I've never seen anyone like that before. I didn't even notice it until I followed him out into the daylight, after we ate together."

It occurred to Rivka that, with all the man's other unnecessary cosmetic fineries, the blue eye -- or even the brown one -- might have been some kind of artificial adjustment. Could someone do that with eyedrops? The frilly cuffs and collar, the jewel-toned, embroidered coat, and his complete apathy about how much money he was spending all pointed to the social class that paid for ridiculous "beauty enhancements," a great measure of which existed solely to indicate the wearer's wealth.

"He must think I'm a mess," Rivka murmured, acutely aware of every tear and stain in her clothing. "You don't care if I'm a mess." She kissed the horse on the bridge of her nose, then rested her head against her. "I'll get us out of this, Dragon, I promise."

Those weren't tears forming. She was watering the horse's nose.

196

Rivka's distress faded easily into determination as she poured herself into her preparation. She walked away from the inn for ten minutes until she found a secluded area behind an overgrown garden fallen into disuse. With her purse, at least full of food now if not money, hanging from a nearby tree, she began the exercises that would help her fully inhabit her own body. Despite all the noise she was making as her feet thumped against the ground and her breath grew loud, she found peace in physical activity. Crunches, bends, and squats were only another language that fit into a lifetime of repetitive prayer.

Getting her head, and her body, in the game was just as much one of her weapons as the sword she carried. Isaac had always taught her not to get distracted, and she was brilliant at keeping even his memory from invading her combat -- or anything *like* combat, either.

The next thing to do was relax, while still keeping her muscles humming. She retrieved her purse and walked back to the built-up area of the city, aware of her skin, her blood, her life force.

Port Saltspray was sinking into a brilliant blue twilight, and the merry glow of torches illuminated all manner of cacophony in the streets. A group of men were brawling outside a gambling establishment, and a nearby policeman didn't seem to care as he eagerly counted out the coins someone in the next building passed over. Rivka's mouth dropped open slightly behind her mask as she realized she'd wound up in the type of town where the local officials were taking bribes on the street without the least concern for who saw.

Wait -- of course they wanted people to see. That way, everyone knows who's in control.

Two women in clothing that was both one notch finer and one notch more revealing than Port Saltspray's custom stood near one of the torches, swishing their skirts slightly each time a man passed them. Before she realized what she was thinking, Rivka had silently evaluated their safety (*Two together will keep each other safer; neither one's face or body language looks terrified or coerced; their clothing is in good repair, so they have some down time or sufficient money; there's no horrifying background man slinking after them in the shadows.*)

These thoughts were all instant and unbidden, the product of her year as a guard for Madam Shayna up north. There she had learned her multiple fighting styles, paying each of the most talented customers in turn to take her out back and give her training, but there she also first found meaning and her place in the world as her strength and her fascination with combat had defended the women who worked there from all manner of predictable threats.

She hoped these ladies had a Rivka of their own or were in some small way their own warrior, at least.

Rivka continued down the streets, people watching and learning the layout so she wouldn't get lost. As she rounded a corner, she heard a distant fiddle. She couldn't make out the tune, but she could tell there was energy in the music.

Through a crowd of people she saw a tiny street musician fiddling in front of a drinking establishment with a large outdoor courtyard. Some of the patrons were clapping along, or stamping their feet, but many of them were too drunk to get the beat right. The fiddler was doing her best to ignore them, playing the most rousing dance rhythm she could.

Rivka swayed slightly and nodded in time. It was perfect; the ideal brain food for the following day. Then she tore herself away and continued her walk.

♡ ✿ ♡

The sun was still pink and hanging over the eastern side of the sea when Rivka rose and began her journey up into the cliffs. The stillness and sweetness of the plants and rocks contrasted sharply with the boisterous city she'd wandered through the night before. Below, a gentle, blue sea flowed in even ripples, and a bird dipped in briefly to retrieve a fish.

She thought about the woman she'd been hired to rescue. Waterweed had warned her that his ladylove didn't speak the language of Port Saltspray but that all Rivka had to do was get her safely back to him and everything would be fine. Rivka judged the idea of a combat for a woman's hand as barbaric, but she hoped that in their barbarism the cliff-dwellers would at least be fair and let her go away with her if she did, in fact, win.

When she won. When she won. Head in the game.

Thoughts of combat blossomed in her mind, and she encouraged them to crowd out all other preoccupations. The physical activity of hiking up the path, which was challenging while not impossibly steep, eased the flow of her thoughts and gave vitality to her memories. She relived fights of her past -- humiliations as well as triumphs, studying from each one as she walked. There was the man who had been obsessed with one of Shayna's employees and refused to leave, and the men who'd come to threaten at the urging of their sister, upset by the frequency of her husband's visits. She thought about the criminals she'd apprehended on the road, or fought off, or narrowly escaped with no more than her life, her horse, and her sword.

It was fun and it was encouraging to think about one's victories, but Rivka knew that one can earn more of them in the future if one is willing also to examine one's defeats. Today was far too important to be afraid of analyzing her weaknesses so that she could learn from them and escape their bindings.

As she approached the top of the cliffs, she began to see more people. Carts in the distance sold food and drink for the spectators, and women were milling about selling bits of cloth stretched out over a frame of sticks to block out the glare of the very direct sun.

Two men overtook her on the trail, and she noted cranky tones in their voices as they spoke to each other. As they passed her, she also observed a familial resemblance.

"Look, there it is. You happy now?"

"I don't see why you have to be so--"

"I don't see why *you* had to come up here with me and enter this thing," said the first man. "This was *my* idea, but you always--"

"--yeah, but this gives us twice the chance of winning!" Rivka got the impression that the second man was the younger of the pair.

"How does that help *me* get a hot piece of tail if you win?"

"We can share!" said the younger one eagerly.

"Ha! You got that from Mother. Share everything, she always said, but what she meant was--"

The brothers walked out of earshot, their argument propelling them to walk faster.

Rivka's blood grew hot and she clenched her fists at her sides, but she channeled her anger into the power she held over her body. One of the most important things Isaac had ever said to her, almost in the same breath as acknowledging their love for the first time, was that she should let her anger work *for* her, not distract her. She would win. She would win, and men like that would be sharing nothing but her dust.

♡ ✿ ♡

"Welcome, welcome, welcome!" A man with a pointed beard and elaborately curled mustache squinted into the crowd of milling warriors. From their clothing and ethnicities, it looked as though they were from all over -- but that really wasn't surprising, considering the constant stream of travelers passing through Port

Saltspray. Rivka tried to stand at what looked like the end of a line, except there were at least five of them. Somehow she got to the front.

She opened her mouth to speak when she finally reached him, but he cut her off. "No swords, please."

"What?"

"Hand-to-hand combat only. We're not trying to kill anyone, just raise some money." He smiled jovially, as though a young woman's bodily autonomy wasn't at stake. Rivka fantasized about drop-kicking him off the side of the cliff and almost heard his imaginary form splash into the water below. Must have been a well-timed wave.

"And why should I feel safe placing my sword in anyone else's care?"

"Come on, northerner!" said Mustachios wearily, waving his hand. "Look around you. You think the people who run this show want to deal with this lot, angry? Everyone will be treated fairly -- we promise."

Except the woman you kidnapped, Rivka grouched inwardly. She remembered that she was on the job, and that she couldn't very well free the woman in the middle of a crowd this big -- especially without her dragon. Frustrated but compliant, she removed her scabbard from her waist. As she handed it over to the man with the mustache, she caught sight of the inscription. It had originally been Isaac's sword, and it still bore his name.

In this land of fraud and crooked police, she had better take no chances. She gave her name to the man as Isaac, just in case. That way, when she came to claim her sword nobody would be able to say she was trying to claim somebody else's.

Too bad -- she liked building up her reputation as Riv, the masked warrior -- but, she could spare Isaac's memory this libation. Especially to keep her sword safe.

When Rivka joined the other warriors around the fence surrounding the fight grounds, she caught her first glimpse of her quarry. The woman whose hand was to be given as the prize for winning today's tournament was seated at the far end of the small field high up on a platform, flanked by enormous guards and tied to the chair with big splashy ribbons that were a grotesque attempt to make the festive out of the frightful.

The captive was around Rivka's age, in her early twenties, and very beautiful. The one part of living as a man that Rivka hadn't mastered was the appeal of courting another woman. She was usually polite but respectfully distant to any who approached her in that regard. But she could still recognize extreme female beauty, and this woman had more than was safe for her, apparently. Her skin was glowing and a pale olive tone, somewhat like Rivka's herself, but her hair was almost black. It fell in dark waves down her shoulders.

She looked thoroughly miserable.

Rivka concentrated on that unhappy face. The other warriors, they were in this to consume her or to prove their worth on the field. Rivka's goal couldn't be more different. This hapless woman might be the rich fiancée of pampered nobility, not the experienced ladies who worked for Madam Shayna, but to Rivka it was the same -- her job was to keep her safe. She wasn't even working strictly for the man who had hired her. Her priorities lay with protecting the woman. So all these other warriors she had to fight today -- what were they, if not just disruptive johns or potential rapists?

It was the same, and she could totally do this. She *had* done this, for over a year, and she knew what she was doing.

202

Rivka looked around at her competition. Some of the men she had never seen before, but she spotted some familiar faces in the crowd. She noticed at least one of the men who had been drinking at the beer garden where she'd stopped to listen to the fiddle player the night before, and was another man definitely one of those from the brawl the officer accepting a bribe had ignored. The brothers who had passed her on the way in were off to her right, arguing over the division of some kind of meat-on-a-stick fair food they had obtained from one of the vendors.

There was a blast of trumpets, and then someone shouted, "Silence for the invocation!"

Rivka felt vaguely out of place as everyone else around her lowered their eyes respectfully and listened as a brass band began to play a local hymn. She knew this part of the world worshipped a pantheon of fascinatingly dysfunctional gods, at least, if the stories she'd picked up were any indication. Rivka usually didn't care, but right now, when everyone else around her was engaged in group prayer, she felt her difference rather pointedly.

Her eyes happened to flicker over to the captive woman on the dais and noticed that she wasn't praying, either.

Then the trumpets blared jubilantly, and the voice shouted again. "On with the combat!"

"Put your hands together for 'Grant Kneecaps,' and the infamous Eustache of Red Tree Shore!" shouted someone else. More trumpets sounded, and Rivka watched the first match while peering intently over the waist-high fence.

"Grant Kneecaps" was the man she recognized from last night's brawl, while Eustache of Red Tree Shore was someone she'd never seen before. She did her best to study both men's fighting styles, especially their strengths and weaknesses, so that she would have some idea of how to handle whichever of them she was to fight.

Rivka was overjoyed when Kneecaps was declared the winner, because now that she'd had two chances to watch him fight, she was fairly confident she could predict his moves. She practically bounded into the ring when they called her in next -- announcing her as Isaac, which she compartmentalized gracefully into oblivion as she put up her fists.

It didn't take her long to defeat him, with the kind of preparation she'd done. Panting, she let the man in charge hold up her hand. The crowd cheered for her, but the only one she cared about, the trapped woman, simply watched in terror.

The announcer called the next fighter into the ring, and Rivka placed him after a moment of thought as one of the men who'd been getting drunk while the fiddler entertained everyone. Thoughts of the beer garden put the fiddler's song back into her mind, and its dancelike rhythm remained with her and kept her energized.

He was an enormous man, tall and fat and muscular. To conquer him and advance, Rivka would need a different strategy. Fortunately, she'd learned more than one way to fight. No matter how large, any living thing has its vulnerable places. As they circled each other in the sand, she aimed for those places, concentrating on them alone, as she used her dexterity as her own defense.

Rivka knew what she was doing, yet avoiding his heavy fists while she took him down took a lot out of her. When he was finally in front of her in the dirt, she was panting heavily, shoulders heaving.

She asked for water and hoped it didn't look like weakness.

They decided to give her a break and let the next pair fight without her. Pouring some of the water over her face after drinking carefully from inside her cloth mask, she watched the two men go at it. One of them was the younger brother from the bickering pair on the path. The other was a bald man with very dark skin and a goatee. Now, *this* was a fight she would have actually had fun watching from the audience -- in another universe where no woman's freedom hung in the balance, of course. They both fought elegantly and with plenty of skill. It was only because of the darker man's age, which likely meant greater experience, that his younger opponent was eventually sent back to the fence in defeat.

Rivka watched the young man rejoin his brother behind the fence. She couldn't hear anything they said to each other over the din of the crowd cheering for the next pair, but they were scowling. She watched the next fight and committed to memory the strengths and weaknesses of each man, as before. When one of them won, a man with mutton-chop sideburns, they called up another fighter who he trounced just as quickly.

"Isaac!" What was that? Oh, they wanted her up again.

She faced down the man with the sideburns, still hearing the fiddle player's music in her mind. She was a machine dedicated to subduing him. He was a threat to that woman over there, no different from a violent customer or an angry, jealous lover.

Rivka won, but that wasn't sweat on her face. Ugh. She hated the taste of blood. *Well, nobody* likes *nosebleeds...* The mask had been stained before, and it would be stained again. It could always be cleaned.

She returned to the throng of warriors outside the fence and found two of them scuffling out of turn. Who knows what insult had initially prompted the quarrel -- now they were going at each other with fists. Guards from the tournament's organizers quickly appeared and broke up the fight, disqualifying both men. Gasps came from the spectators as one of the guards produced a knife from one of the delinquent's shoes.

"No blades in the ring!" bellowed the man in charge as he pocketed the knife for himself. "That goes for everyone who's left! We find anything else like this, the whole thing's off!"

205

The remaining contestants eyed each other uneasily.

The older brother was up next, and she watched him defeat someone she didn't recognize. Then he fought the darker man who had eliminated his brother. Rivka watched the fight with great interest and in some instances had to remind herself to breathe. Both men fought with a skill that fascinated her. It would have been nice to learn from them, or even spar with them for fun.

If they weren't trying to force someone into marriage.

What was wrong with the world?

Finally, the lighter-skinned man won on a technicality when the darker man's shoe came apart.

"Not fair!" screamed half the crowd.

"Sucks to be you!" jeered the other half.

Rivka studied her own worn and tattered shoes uneasily. When she looked up again, she realized that she and the older brother were the only ones left.

She pursed her lips beneath the mask. From the bout she'd just witnessed, neither he nor his opponent had any major flaws in their fighting style, nor were they terrifically predictable or gave easy tells to their next move.

Well, she'd just have to move beyond fighting as her strategy, then.

"You fight well," she said as she approached him in the center of the ring.

He nodded sharply. "Thank you. You too. Your nose okay?"

Even though his tone was gentle, she could tell he was trying to psych her out by referring to the patch of blood spreading across her mask. *You don't know that I'm a woman, and women are used to the sight of blood. I could show you four times as much blood soon. Just hang around for about, oh, two weeks. I'll bleed on everything you love.*

"You know, your younger brother's a pretty good fighter too," she pointed out, trying to sound casual. "I bet your mother's really proud of both of you. You should be nicer to him. I bet he looks up to you a lot."

"Oh, is *that* what you think?"

The trumpets sounded, and the fight began. And, just as Rivka had intended, her opponent began to fight badly. It wasn't that she had thrown him off his game or distracted him. The simple fact was, by evoking his little brother, she had tricked him into unconsciously seeing her as his brother's stand-in, and fighting her as if he fought against his brother's techniques. He knew his brother all too well. He didn't know anything about Rivka beyond today's arena, and she executed every technique that ran completely counter to the ones his little brother had used.

The best part was, he didn't even know where he was going wrong. He didn't realize why his responses were off -- they just were.

By the time he got his mind in the game, all he could do was hurt Rivka's body -- not her chances of winning. She wore her pain like a rooster wears his brilliant tail feathers, like something she could shuck off if she chose. He could kick all he wanted. She was winning. She had won.

Rivka had forgotten about the nosebleed and, as was her habit, wiped the sweat off her face from underneath her mask. Her hand came out bloody, and this was the hand that the man in charge held up to the crowd to cheer for her. She couldn't help but laugh at the theatrical display.

They placed a garland of woven paper around her neck and led her, panting and sweating and covered in sand, to the chair where the captive woman sat. "Meet your new husband, Isaac," said someone to her left, and someone on her right repeated again to the woman, "Isaac."

Rivka was glad for her mask, for explaining her profound frown would have been impossible. Oh, if only irony were another warrior she could beat up in the middle of the field!

"This is great, but can I go clean up somewhere and get my sword back?" she asked her handlers.

Deferentially and full of respect, they led her to a mountain stream. Somebody brought back her sword while she scrubbed away at the blood and dirt. She gave them each a small bread roll from her purse. It seemed appropriate.

Those attending her were joined by the man with the curled mustache. "Congratulations, young stallion from the north!"

Stop. Talking. "Thank you, sir," said Rivka.

"Right this way." He escorted her to a small tent, high up on the rocks. "Your bride awaits you inside."

"I see. Can we leave soon?"

"Whenever you like!" He was just as amiable as before. Was he thinking not at all of the humanity of the woman inside -- of her fear, her despair, her entrapment? "Is there anything I can bring you to make you more comfortable?"

"No, please -- actually, I'd like privacy." She knew what he would think, but let him. Let it work for her. Let them get as far as they could from this place -- especially now that she had "the right."

First thing, though, she wanted to give the woman her own choice. Money was a good thing, and she needed it to free her horse. Yet she'd rather have done all that fighting for no pay, she'd rather be forced to follow in her father's footsteps and work in the fields for a month, than accept money for bringing a woman to a man she didn't want. Most likely, the dark-haired beauty really was his fiancée and missed him terribly, and longed for their reunification, but Rivka didn't want to assume. She'd seen too much of the world. After all, plenty of women became betrothed to men for someone else's convenience.

She squared her shoulders and stepped inside.

The brunette shrank back several feet when she saw her, eyes blazing, and Rivka stopped moving so she wouldn't appear a threat. Now that they had privacy, Rivka was desperate for the other woman to feel safe and to trust her. She didn't have to make sure she was watching her -- those huge brown eyes, frightened but proud, were fixed squarely upon her. So Rivka carefully and deliberately took a step backward, bowed her head, and then knelt on one knee. She bowed her head again and then looked back up at the woman.

The strings that seemed to be holding the brunette's body tense in every direction released themselves. She bowed her head slightly, returning the greeting. *"Forse sei un uomo onesto. Potresti riportarmi da mia zia?"* She spoke with the air of a queen, but Rivka had absolutely no idea what she was saying.

"I'm sorry, I don't speak--" Rivka stopped talking, realizing how futile the words were. She pointed to her ear, and then her mouth, and then shook her head. The woman looked troubled, so Rivka added, "Riv," and pointed to herself. "Riv."

"Stella."

Rivka bowed her head again in acknowledgment.

"Ma, pensavo che il tuo nome fosse Isaac?" Then Stella's distress flickered for a moment as she let out a half-chuckle as if

laughing at herself for trying again talk to the warrior who clearly couldn't understand.

Rivka caught the name in her question, didn't know how to mime an explanation for using the other name during the contest, and simply nodded. Fine, then -- she would be both of them.

From the look in Stella's eyes, she was intensely thinking. "Isaac -- Abraham, Isaac, Jacob?" she recited.

That was a familiar litany -- the three names of the patriarchs! Rivka's heart quickened.

"Sarah--"

"--*Rivka*, Rachel, Leah," Rivka finished the names of the four matriarchs with her, heat flooding into her cheeks. Stella worshipped as she did! This was a starting place, because now she knew that even if the languages of their everyday lives weren't the same, they prayed in the same tongue.

Not that this instantly cleared up all difficulties. It didn't do a great deal of good to be able to praise God together a thousand different ways if she couldn't actually communicate about mortal life and its dangers.

Stella stepped closer, took her hand, and motioned for her to stand again. When she spoke again, it was in the language of prayer. "*Hear, my people, the Lord is our God; the Lord is one.*" She wasn't praying -- it was a test.

"*Blessed is God's glorious majesty for ever and ever,*" Rivka answered by rote. She'd certainly never expected to be using the Sh'ma as a password, and this moment had far more to do with the urgencies of the mortal world than any spiritual place. But life on the road was all about using all the weapons in your quiver, even the ones you forgot you had, or didn't think would ever serve.

She pointed at Stella.

"Stella," said Stella, nodding.

Rivka shook her head and pointed to her again.

"*Il mio...*" Stella replied, seeming to comprehend finally that Rivka meant to talk about something *of* hers, rather than her specifically.

Next, Rivka referenced the prayer that ushered in the hours of Shabbat, which starts with *Come, beloved*. "Beloved."

Stella furrowed her brow and shook her head.

Rivka cocked her head in question, but Stella dropped her hand and held both of her own up in the air, shaking her head harder.

No beloved? "Bride?" she tried, which was another word from the Sabbath prayer.

Stella shook her head again.

"Beloved," said Rivka again, then showed Stella her purse, then pointed to herself. *Your beloved paid me.*

For a third time, Stella shook her head. She pointed to herself, smiled as she shook her head as she repeated, "Beloved." She had no beloved, and she was happy to have none. Then she shrugged, her hands in the air again, and shook her head. She was happy if she would never have one.

Rivka pointed to her purse again, and Stella's face grew questioning. Rivka looked around the tent for a moment, then realized Stella's dress had plenty of blue in it. She pointed to one of her eyes, then to the dress. Then she pointed to her other eye. She didn't even have to finish pointing to her own brown clothing before a change came over Stella that startled even a seasoned warrior like Rivka.

Fear pulsing through her face, Stella jumped back, shaking. "*Vetro colorato! Il diavolo di vetro colorato!*" She stepped closer

211

to Rivka again and seized both of her hands, shaking her head violently.

"Okay, so not your fiancé, then," Rivka muttered to herself in her own language.

Stella looked deeply into her eyes and chose from their legends the one name they'd all been trained since childhood to fear, the villain who'd wanted them all dead, whose name the children blotted out with noisemakers every time the legend was told. "Haman."

Rivka needed a moment. The food in her purse felt like poison, and she suddenly wanted to set it all on fire and kick it off the side of the cliff.

Well, that wouldn't do anybody any good. She needed to tell Stella that everything was going to be okay. In her mind, she grasped at the legends.

Rivka knew she couldn't say *Esther* while preserving the fiction of her maleness. Besides, there was a better match, even though he was from a different story -- a figure who had led his people to freedom. She pointed to herself and said, "Moses."

♡ ✡ ♡

Stella visibly relaxed when Rivka had gotten her away from her abductors on the cliff. "Leah? Leah, Rachel, Joseph," Stella said as they began the hike back down the cliff to Port Saltspray. She was pointing to herself at "Joseph." Then she pointed back down the cliff at the scurrying inhabitants of the port. "Leah." She was using the relationships of people in the old stories to explain who was waiting for her in the city.

"Your aunt is down there," Rivka interpreted to herself in her own tongue. Clearly, Stella was a niece and not a nephew, but Rivka couldn't think of any aunt-and-niece pairs in their common legends, and she surmised that Stella probably couldn't, either, especially on demand.

Next, Stella pointed to herself, then pointed over to the ocean. No -- not to the ocean, her pointing finger was arched upward, as if she meant "across the sea."

"Zembluss?"

Stella nodded vigorously.

Rivka pointed at herself and then to the far north.

Stella nodded again in understanding.

Stella was keeping pace with her pretty well, but she was breathing heavily even over easy ground. Rivka found a flattish rock and patted it, indicating that Stella could sit down and rest for a little. Stella practically collapsed onto it, and Rivka realized she didn't know the last time Stella had eaten.

Rivka took another bread roll out of her purse and offered it over. Stella accepted it gratefully and inhaled it in two bites, almost choking in her eagerness. Next, Rivka gave her a swig from her canteen.

Soon, Stella was feeling well enough to continue, and she hopped back on her feet and started back down the trail.

Rivka made sure to let Stella rest more now that it had clicked in her mind that she needed it. She also kept her eyes peeled for native plants that looked edible, although so close to the sea there wasn't much. The only thing she found were the salty green stems that crunched like a vegetable, but Stella wasn't choosy and nibbled at them as they walked.

The women also passed the time teaching each other their culture's word for *bird*, *tree*, and whatever else was easy to indicate by pointing. Rivka concentrated on committing the newfound language to memory, since she was trying to travel to Zembluss for her next career move.

As the walk unfolded, she was preoccupied with how different it was to carry on an everyday conversation in a language she'd previously only used for prayer. A lifetime of weekly religious services had given her no way to ask questions about Stella's life or to entertain her with stories of her own adventures on the road.

There were people far away, even farther south than Zembluss, who spoke this language every day -- they used it to buy fruit at the marketplace and have arguments over the weather and ask their sweethearts to marry them. Rivka thought about them now and wondered if she'd make it that far south in her journeys.

Still, there were some conversations that could be cobbled together from prayer words. "Beloved?" Stella asked, looking at Rivka curiously and pointing to her as she spoke. "Bride?"

Coming from some women, Rivka felt a special weight in questions like that, since she was posing as a man. Not so from Stella. Her questions and her presence felt simply like friendship.

Part of the services for the yearly Day of Atonement, just after New Year's, contained a line about "those who perish in fire." That would have been a perfect explanation, but when Rivka scraped around in her mind for the words, she could only remember them in her own language. Instead, Rivka answered about Isaac by reciting the beginning of the mourning prayer. *"Exalted and hallowed be God's great name in the world which God created, according to plan."*

Stella looked a little bit shocked, but reached her hand over and squeezed Rivka's in comfort.

♡ ✿ ♡

"I can't thank you enough. You wouldn't believe how much I've given this town's useless police in bribes, but of course it didn't do any good. I didn't know where next to turn!" Stella's aunt had a heavy accent, but at least she could speak the local language. She and Rivka were standing in the back garden of a small but expensive inn that overlooked the water.

"Tell me about the war in Zembluss," said Rivka. "I was hoping to get passage there with my horse -- I hear both sides are looking for mercenaries."

"It's a terrible thing, terrible." The older woman's face darkened. "Theaters turned into garrisons, women no longer safe in the streets -- I've lost so many friends. Some have died, but others -- monsters for one side or for the other. It was all I could do to get away with Stella and start over."

"I promise I won't be the kind of soldier who makes the land unsafe for its own women." Sometimes Rivka's heart hurt.

"Yes, I know that." Stella's aunt took both Rivka's hands in hers. "If Stella wanted a husband, I'd want for her someone like you."

"Thank you, of course," said Rivka with a tone of extreme deference. "So I understood her correctly that she doesn't want marriage? We spoke on the cliffs, but we weren't always communicating."

"No, she really doesn't ever want to get married!" said the aunt. "I even thought, you know, maybe she doesn't like a man, then she can have a female companion. I had someone like that once. But no, not even that... she says she's complete with family and friends."

"There's all kinds of people in the world," Rivka agreed. "Will she be safe now?"

"She needs to learn the language; this much, it is certain. But maybe she will learn another language instead. This is not a good place to settle." The woman picked idly at a stray rose petal, which was spoiling on a nearby bush and about to fall off its flower anyway. "We will move on, to a safer town, with better police."

"I think that's the best decision," said Rivka. "It will take a lot to clean this place up."

"It's not all terrible," said Stella's aunt. She cupped one of the roses on the bush in her hand and dragged it, still growing on its stem, closer to Rivka. "Smell this."

Rivka bent down and filled her nose with fragrance. She allowed herself this moment of luxury, then stood up straight once again. The job wasn't done yet.

"Tell me about the man who hired me."

♡ ✿ ♡

Half past midnight, a masked figure astride a dragon flew to the top floor of Port Saltspray's most exclusive hotel. Seizing the fancy molded windows, on which sculpted representations of dolphins cavorted through the town's eponymous salt spray, Rivka easily swung herself inside. She left the dragon -- ransomed tonight with money from Stella's grateful aunt -- plastered against the side of the building like a gargantuan moth, and crept with practiced silence toward the man sleeping on his back in the bed before her.

With calculating suddenness, she seized his right arm and pinned it to the mattress.

He awoke instantly and reached for something under his pillow with his left hand. But she'd anticipated this and flipped the dagger from his hand just as quickly as he wielded it. He glared up at her with one blue eye and one brown as she squatted on his chest.

"Thank you for confirming for me that you can use your left arm," Rivka growled. "So can I." Still holding him down with her right arm, she socked him hard with her left fist.

216

"What's the matter with you? You missed our rendezvous." He looked up at her dispassionately, trying to trick her with a disarming tone. "What do you care about my arm? I would have paid you handsomely."

"To help you kidnap an innocent woman, you mean!" Rivka shook him and dug her heel into his gut. "I am nobody's pawn. She wasn't your fiancée at all, you *chazzer*. She was an innocent woman you tried to use me to help kidnap, to ransom or to rape -- or both. You recognized her and her aunt as Zembluss nobility who came here to get away from the civil war, and figured she'd be easy pickings, especially when someone else had already done the hard part."

"Ooh, it knows how to talk," the man taunted.

"Is that all you think I am -- hired brawn with no head?" Rivka shouted. "Maybe you should be the one with no head."

"Maybe you should be the one with no *tongue*," the man retorted in a threatening whisper, struggling against her.

"But then you had to find a patsy, someone to do the work for you. You wore that fancy coat two sizes too big, knowing it would make you look like a weakling if it didn't fit, and you approached the first desperate thug you could find -- or so you thought. You couldn't go up into the mountains yourself and enter the fight because everyone in the mountain clan has a price on your head. Just like both sides of the war in Zembluss do." Rivka snorted. "I don't know why -- I wouldn't pay for something that ugly."

"You're no prize yourself, barbarian."

"*Exactly.*" Her voice was bearlike; she had claws to match. "But you made a big mistake when you drew attention to yourself with me. *I want that bounty.* I need money far too badly to be scared of your reputation, Stained-Glass Devil."

The man chuckled. "Oh, they told you about me?"

"Stella's aunt told me everything -- your crimes back in Zembluss, what you've been up to since you came here... I made her stop. I only have time to hear about so much rape and murder in one day."

"Then the old bitch should have warned you to *stay on your guard*!" At that, the man sprang up like an arrow launched from a bowstring.

Rivka *was* on her guard, but he was a fierce adversary. She'd come in here expecting a fight, but she'd never fought someone so terrifyingly cavalier about his own safety before. He'd rather he get hurt as long as it enabled him to hurt her. She was gladder than ever that she'd made sure to ask Stella's opinion first before simply bringing her down to him like a butcher's boy with a sack of lamb chops.

She unsheathed her sword, but he kicked it away, and it landed on the other side of the room with a dull clang. She glanced out at the window as best she could, but the dragon had vanished. Most likely, her mysteriously waning powers had necessitated a trip back down to the ground so that she could collapse back into her horse form without plummeting to her death. Not that she could have been much help even as a dragon -- there was no way she could have fit inside the window anyway.

Rivka poured all her best techniques into fighting the Stained-Glass Devil, but somehow he got the better of her and both his hands wound up around her throat. She kicked at him and tried to pull his hands away, but he was evidently used to this. Blood thundered in her head, and a wave of naked panic ripped through her.

But she had come into this room expecting to fight, whereas he'd been asleep, and she was still one step ahead of him. Out from where she'd stashed it came the dagger he'd kept under his

218

pillow, the one he'd tried to use on her when she'd first roused him. She drove it into the side of his throat.

He let out a horrid little noise and released her, clutching at the wound.

In his final seconds, she grabbed her cloth mask and ripped it from her face in anger. "Here's the woman I promised you."

The Stained-Glass Devil fell to the floor, dead. Rivka stood at his body, breathing heavily and pawing at her mauled windpipe. She was unmasked, and she was thoroughly spattered with the blood of the man she'd killed. This was how the dragon found Rivka when she returned to the window, her strength renewed.

"Oh, there you are, you big goof," said Rivka. It was hard to talk. "Hey, I need your help with him."

Rivka lounged in the beer garden, dressed in the finest set of leather armor she could find. She had made herself another mask and even treated herself to new underthings. In front of her was the world's biggest pile of chicken livers, some carrot sticks providing a hilariously ineffective protest against decadence, and a tankard of something dark and sweet and strong.

Nearby, the fiddle player from the other day was sitting on the curb eagerly eating chicken wings. Rivka had bought them for her in appreciation of the inspiration she'd provided on the night before the fight. Before the *many* fights.

And, best of all, the horse-dragon-something Rivka called her best friend was standing just outside the beer garden, swishing her tail at the flies and watching Rivka eat.

She leaned her chair backward precariously and fed the horse a carrot stick. The beast deserved as many carrots as Rivka deserved chicken livers; this morning after flying Rivka back up the mountain to claim the bounty on her midnight capture, she'd stood guard in her dragon form as the exhausted warrior slept for hours on a secluded area of the beach. But even if she hadn't, Rivka was gladder than anything to have won her freedom.

And Rivka made quite the impression up there on the cliff face too! Yesterday, she'd trudged in on foot, in dusty clothing, one of over half a dozen warriors who all looked as fearsome as she. Today, she'd ridden in just before dawn, blood-spattered, confident, and otherworldly, on the back of a dragon. Many of the mountain folk had only seen dragons before in the distance, out over the sea as the more marine-oriented of the beasts hunted dolphins. Now the people hid behind the trees, peering at her, their voices a rumble of fascination as they chattered about her and gawked at her great black-green beast. Dragon was large enough to carry three people on her back, and Rivka heard more than one of them compare her wings to the fins of a swordfish.

This time, as she handed over the body of the man who had come all the way from Zembluss to cause them so much grief, she gave them her real name, Riv. They would be talking for years of the mysterious masked warrior with two names, who had arrived one morning to win a combat tournament and came back when it was barely the next to deliver their most-wanted criminal.

Now at rest, Rivka gazed out across the port's main road to the restless blue water, sparkling in a thousand places from the late-afternoon sun. Between the reward from Stella's aunt and the bounty on the notorious Stained-Glass Devil, within the span of three days she'd gone from being so broke she couldn't pay attention to having more money than she knew what to do with.

Scratch that. She knew *exactly* what to do with it.

As soon as practically possible, Rivka and her dragon were getting their *tuchuses* out of Port Saltspray.

END

Aviva and the Aliens

With appreciation to Kristen for her help, and with love to Spouseling.

It was the ninth month of the reign of Queen Shulamit. The litchi trees were in full bloom, and the people of Perach were getting ready for Passover. All across the country, children helped their parents scrub the whole house down to make sure no stray particles had escaped spring-cleaning. Everyone was working hard to get her kitchen completely bread-free.

Everyone except Aviva, of course, whose kitchen was already the most bread-free place in the land.

Even so, Aviva still had plenty of work to do. Her market bags were still on her table, brimming over with a bounty ranging from turmeric root to salty, chewy cheese to fresh peas. Everything needed to be sorted and put away so that she would have plenty of time tomorrow to get ready for the royal seder. The Head Cook, with her army of helpers in the palace's main kitchen, would oversee most of the food, but everything that touched the queen's lips had to come from Aviva's kitchen.

Including me, thought Aviva with a grin. Queen Shulamit was an eager connoisseur of her kisses and her cooking alike.

Thunder rumbled outside, and Aviva felt safe and secure inside the kitchen-house. It wasn't a big deal if she got stuck here for a little bit while she started to prep for tomorrow night. It was already nighttime -- in fact, Shulamit was knocked out in bed early, sleeping off a heavy day of hearing cases in court -- so the sky outside the window could give no indication of how bad the storm would be.

Even so, there was something strange about the visible night. Aviva, holding the turmeric root in one hand, paused in her work to glance out the window. The air outside looked strangely still, if indeed a storm was coming on.

222

Aviva brushed stray wisps of black hair out of her face and returned to her work. As she emptied the first bag of its contents, she spotted something unexpected way down at the bottom. She brought the tiny sack over to the lamp to read the note attached to the small cloth pouch. *"For Aviva -- thank you for your business and Chag Sameach. A little something in case you run short in your baking."* The pouch was made of the same cloth as everything else that came from the spice man, so she inferred he must have slipped it into her bag between the star anise and coriander seeds.

Wondering eagerly what kind of spice was in the unexpected gift, Aviva opened the pouch and sniffed.

Flour!

She froze, momentarily stunned. It wasn't a spice at all. It was extra flour for matzo. The folks in the marketplace didn't entirely understand why she was so careful when she bought the raw materials for the queen's food, and even the ones who did usually dismissed Shulamit's problems as the pickiness of royalty. They, of course, hadn't been the one standing there holding her braids out of the way while she threw up, or holding her gently as she tried to sleep off stomach cramps.

Aviva forgave easily. Even in error, the flour was a kind gesture. And since it was still in the bag, it was easy to seal it back up again. No harm done. She'd just take it to the main kitchen and see if the head cook needed it for anything.

Resting the pouch of flour against a calabash, she finished emptying the bags of star anise, coriander, and peppercorns into their respective jars to join their companions. Then, feeling rushed by the sound of another boom of thunder, she rose, took the bag of flour in hand, and opened the door to the kitchen-house.

And yelped.

Gone were the palm trees and vegetable garden that wrapped all the way around the house; gone was the balmy night sky. Instead, she'd opened the door into a vast, gray wasteland lit by sickly white lights. The ground looked like stone -- no, like hard, compacted sand. The sky -- no, that wasn't a sky, that was a *ceiling* -- and walls were made of dull silver metal.

She was inside of something. Her entire kitchen-house had been plucked out of the palace courtyard and transported inside... what?

Maybe that's why she'd heard thunder without seeing any wind. Maybe it wasn't thunder at all.

Aviva didn't see anyone in the big gray chamber, but she wasn't taking any chances. Placing the sack of flour carefully on the table next to the calabash again, she retrieved one of her sharpest knives from her knife block.

She was just in time. A door opened at the far end of the gray chamber, and two *beings* stepped through it and moved toward her.

They were tall and thin and looked like no people she'd ever seen. Gigantic eyes shone like glass bowls full of black water from the crown of oblong heads, and while they walked on two legs, they had four arms instead of two. Their skin looked slick and shiny, if it was even skin, and reminded her of tiger's-eye the way it shone back and forth between brown and black.

They wore belts with strange objects hanging from them, and small white spheres were strapped to their throats with bits of cord. One of the strangers was also sporting a cylinder of brilliant blue on its head and carried itself with the pride of a leader.

"Zzzzggghhhtt plbbbbbttt mmmmooooooop," said the one wearing the hat.

"Turn on your language box, Commander," said the other one deferentially.

The commander fiddled with the box on its necklace and then spoke again. "Is it working now?"

"Yes, sir."

"Good. You there!" This time he was calling to Aviva. "Can you understand me?"

"I can," she called loudly, her left hand on her hip and her right firmly clasping her knife. "If you can understand me, send me home right away."

"We have come a long way," said the commander. "Our world is five thousand *kadrooms* from yours."

"I don't know what that means," said Aviva.

"Our sun is nothing but one of the stars in the sky to you," explained the subordinate. "As yours is to us."

"If you're foreigners, then maybe you're unfamiliar with our customs," said Aviva. "We don't steal strangers out of their homes, and we don't steal their homes, either!"

"Our spaceship has been traveling for seven *bayzoms*," said the commander grandiosely, "and our food replicators are worthless!"

"I don't know what a *bayzom* is, either," said Aviva. "Are you sure those boxes are working?"

"It means we're sick of eating flavorless protein coagulants!" shouted the commander. His shiny eyes became even shinier, apparently in reaction to his heightened agitation.

"If you dock your spaceship in our city, there are plenty of places to get food in exchange for money or work," said Aviva, "but you can't just barge in and take a whole person!"

225

"Who will stop us?"

Aviva sputtered and gestured at her knife. "I will! Besides, I'm the last person you want to mess with. I'm the queen's personal chef, and she's best friends with a warrior hero and a dragon. Do you know what a dragon is?"

"No," said the commander, "but unless it can travel through space, I don't see how it concerns us. You're in orbit, Chef."

"What do you mean?"

"You're up in the air. You're *yidrees* above your planet," said the subordinate.

"Unless this dragon of yours can travel through your planet's atmosphere and the vacuum of space, you're all alone up here with us," said the commander.

Aviva's eyes widened as she looked from one to the other. Her hand tightened on her knife. "Please let me go back to my family."

"Cook us dinner first."

She looked at the commander suspiciously. "That's all?" Aviva knew more of humanity's evils than she cared to think about. Then again, these weren't exactly humanity. She realized what animal they reminded her of -- locusts. They looked like giant locusts.

Wearing belts.

"What could be more important than a good meal?" The commander threw up his top set of hands in a gesture that looked like a shrug while the bottom set of hands reached for her. "Do you have anything you need? We tried to take your entire kitchen."

"You did," Aviva answered with a sigh, looking around her stores. Well, she supposed she could make a quick stir-fry... "Will I have access to water if I run out?"

"What is water?"

"Dihydrogen monoxide, Commander," answered the subordinate.

"Ah, yes, yes. Wonderful stuff. We worship it, you know."

Aviva was only half listening. The sooner she could get a meal together, the sooner she'd be safe at home and reunited with her family. It was interesting to think about what that meant to her -- to be home. After all, they'd taken her kitchen-house with her, so technically, she was still "home." But that wasn't true at all, because to her, home was where Queen Shulamit was, where she could listen admiringly as the queen ran her mouth a mile a minute about trade disputes or legal points or advances in peach cultivation, where she could be there to take a soft hand in hers and massage out the stress of the day by working at each finger one at a time. Home was Shulamit's awkward smile as she saw what new inventions Aviva had cooked up for her that day, and home was watching her grow into her father's throne with new capabilities every day.

Cook your heart out, Chef, Aviva told herself, *and get home.*

She found something to measure with and began to pour out rice. "Neither of you two gets sick from any foods, do you?"

The subordinate locust-man came to the door of the kitchen-house. "What?"

"Some people get ill if they eat the wrong foods," said Aviva. She dumped the rice into a pot, then began to measure water from the basin she'd filled earlier in the day.

"Sometimes the commander eats too many *bep-beps* and has to lie down and drink liquid infused with gas," said the subordinate in a conversational tone.

"What is -- never mind." Aviva shook her head. "But that's from eating too many, right? Not from a small amount?"

"Yes, from too many."

"That's not the same thing. We'll be fine." Her fingers worked at cloves of garlic, freeing them of their delicate skins. The action was familiar enough to soothe her, at least a little. She'd been shucking garlic her whole life, or peeling carrots, or shelling peas, so at least she still felt like herself. She thought of Shulamit again, sleeping in her royal bedchamber with her braids undone and her thick, black hair spilling across the embroidered pillowcases. Aviva's fingers worked faster. Hopefully, she'd be able to get home before Shulamit woke up and found her missing. She'd left once before, on purpose, and she hoped Shulamit trusted her enough now to send Captain Rivka after her instead of thinking she'd run off again.

"You're good at that!" said the subordinate.

"Thanks," said Aviva, dicing onions with dazzling alacrity.

"You've been doing it your whole life?"

Aviva nodded.

"I can tell. You are, then, worker class?"

Aviva simply grunted. That was a complicated question; yes, she was working class, and proud of it, but she was also the queen's romantic companion, so her life was privileged in certain obvious ways. She also didn't see why she should have to make trivial conversation with her kidnappers -- especially when there was work to be done.

228

"I am not worker class. I am merchant class," said the subordinate proudly.

"Are you?" said Aviva in her best bored voice. She retrieved a skinny purple eggplant from one of her baskets and began slicing it into discs.

"I am merchant class and I am not married."

"Hm," said Aviva. Suddenly, the eggplant was *fascinating*. She simply could not take her eyes from it.

"Are you married?"

The question shouldn't have caught Aviva off guard the way that it did. No, she was not married, but she was married to Shulamit in her heart. What was that called? Everybody in the palace understood it; those outside the palace either understood also or chose to ignore it. Women who took each other as partners were often invisible in their society; she hoped that someday she and Shulamit would be a reason for that custom to give way to a new one in which all consensual adult relationships could be celebrated and recognized.

Her hesitation gave her away. "Are you looking for a husband, then?" The subordinate took a tiny but threatening step closer.

Aviva lifted her knife under the pretext of chopping more vegetables, but she aimed a steely gaze right at him. "No, I'm not."

"You are mated, then? What does he do? Is he also worker class?"

Aviva, still holding her knife, put both hands on her hips and gave him a withering look. "No, *she's* the queen of the whole country. Is that enough class for you?"

"A woman? Do you not like men?"

229

"There are some men that I like -- I just like her best." Aviva knew it was probably smarter to pretend she didn't like any men, but she also wasn't the type to hide behind potted plants. Nobody should have to.

"But if you like men, then you are still in need of a husband. I would like to volunteer--"

"To help me shell peas? Sounds great! Here you go." Aviva practically threw the pouch of fresh peas at his head, then turned her back to him completely. She had a good-sized rear, and she hoped he was getting the idea from having it replace her face as his conversational companion.

To keep him from talking any more, she started to sing. Since tomorrow was the first night of Passover -- if she could get home for it -- she started with 'One Baby Goat.' It helped keep her sane and created the illusion of a shell of autonomy around her body while she worked.

Soon, the joyous odor of star anise, coriander, and cinnamon filled the air. With a flourish, Aviva sprinkled a handful of sesame seeds over her pan, stepped back, and declared it finished. "Food's ready!"

The commander and his subordinate waited patiently at a table at the edge of the gray chamber with both sets of hands resting in their laps, the top set covering the bottom ones, as she dished out the food. Each of them got a big plate of white rice topped with fresh and colorful stir-fried vegetables. The eggplant was tender; the peas were bright green and cheerful; the fresh cilantro on the side of the plate evoked memories of the garden she usually had right outside her doorstep.

Aviva stood in the corner and watched them while they ate. They seemed happy enough, which made her relax some of the muscles she hadn't even realized she was tensing. Her thoughts wandered to the seder happening in the palace the following night. Aviva's parents had moved into the palace -- one of those perks of being the queen's "favorite" -- and she was looking forward to impressing them with her professional handiwork. She was also looking forward to hearing Shulamit lead a royal seder for the first time. She'd only been queen since last fall; King Noach was still alive last Passover.

Aviva had a sobering thought: Shulamit would probably need extra comforting tomorrow night, as memories of past seders made her miss her father worse than usual. Aviva longed to be with her, to cover her in generous hugs.

"This is wonderful, Earth woman!"

"Thank you, Commander," said Aviva, approaching the table. She was still holding her knife. After the kind of experiences she'd had in her life, she wasn't about to put it down. Especially after the way the subordinate locust-man had talked to her.

"*Beeeeeeeeeezit blarrrgh boom.*" The Commander had turned to face the other one, and Aviva realized he had turned off his language box. Immediately suspicious, she gripped the knife harder and felt adrenaline marinate through her body.

The subordinate smiled, and his big, glassy eyes rotated slightly in his head.

With a touch to his throat to reactivate his language box, the commander turned back to Aviva. "Very good food. You will stay with us and continue to cook us good food."

"No," said Aviva assertively, "I'm going back to the palace with my family."

"How are you going to get there?" queried the commander.

"You'll take me back. You have to take me back," Aviva insisted. "I cooked for you, just as you asked!"

The commander shrugged. "That was an audition."

"No, it was *not*." Aviva hurried behind him and put her knife to his throat. "Take. Me. Home. Aaaa!" she yelped, for the subordinate had aimed one of the weird things on his belt at her knife. It zapped into nonexistence. "My knife! You pile of toads -- I'm a chef! You took my knife! *Never* mess with a chef's knives."

The subordinate responded by zapping her with the weird thing instead. Her arm stung as if she'd been whipped. Breathing heavily, she looked back and forth from one locust man to the other, fear and caution mixing with her growing hatred.

"As you can see, we really aren't scared of you," said the commander dispassionately. He was still finishing his food.

"What if I refuse to cook?" Aviva shot back.

"Ensign, turn on the view screen." The commander finished his order with a loud burp, which Aviva could smell. She wrinkled her nose and fantasized about Captain Rivka punching his stupid face in.

The subordinate -- the ensign -- stood up and hit a button on the wall. A panel slid away, revealing a black surface that reminded her of dull matte satin. She figured that's what they meant by 'view screen.' He hit another button, and an image of the slumbering queen appeared before them. Aviva gasped at the unexpected technology. "Where is she?" She also felt an illogical burst of protectiveness about Shulamit's *hair*, of all things -- seeing her with her braids down was not something reserved for just anybody!

"She's asleep in her bed, down on the planet," said the commander. "But we can easily zap her, just as we did your knife."

Aviva stood completely still, unable to breathe. All of her bluster had been knocked out of her. If they'd vanished her knife so easily, could they really do that to a person? Maybe they were bluffing -- but then, her arm still smarted from where Ensign Jerkface had gotten her a few moments ago. Even if that's all they could do to Shulamit, she couldn't do anything that would make it happen.

And what if they really could kill her?

For a moment, Aviva imagined herself leaving with them, selflessly putting away her own needs yet again, as she had all through her childhood during her mother's illness, and as she had as an adult last year when she'd left Shulamit the first time to save her mother's health. She imagined a loveless existence, up in this floating stone prison, cooking for people she hated, with God for her only companion. She imagined cherishing her loved ones, forever taken from them, knowing they'd never imagine why she'd disappeared. She imagined Shulamit trying to lead the royal seder for the first time tomorrow night with tears flowing down her cheeks, choking her until she couldn't get the words out.

Seder...

"Tomorrow night is one of our biggest holidays," Aviva told the aliens quietly.

"What do you celebrate?" asked the commander.

"I'll tell you the story later," she continued with unnatural calm, "and when I tell you, I will feed you the ceremonial food that all of our people eat with the Passover meal."

"You aren't trying to poison us to get away, are you?" asked the commander suspiciously.

"Because we have your queen in our sights!" the ensign reminded her.

"I can see that," said Aviva. "And no, no poison. I promise. Everyone in our kingdom eats it." Everyone except for Shulamit, but she didn't want to get into that.

She turned to go back into the kitchen-house. "I'll let you know when it's ready."

Gritting her teeth, she set to work. It would mean having to reclean the kitchen, even if it worked, but if that meant getting to be reunited with her family again, it was definitely worth it. And with a wry grin, Aviva realized that, in a way, she was glad that her kitchen would need to be scrubbed clean alongside her fellow countrymen's. She supposed that it was only fitting that she participate in the holiday fully like everybody else.

She picked up the bag of flour and concentrated on her task.

Sometime later, Aviva emerged from the kitchen-house carrying a plate of large, square crackers. "We call this matzo," she told the aliens.

The commander eyed the plate with interest. "What is its purpose?"

"To celebrate Passover," said Aviva. "It's all about freedom. And I promise it's not poison." To demonstrate, she picked up the top square and broke off a corner piece.

When they saw her eat, the commander and the ensign both visibly relaxed. They each took a square off the plate and took a hearty bite.

"Uggh!"

"Is this a joke?"

"What is this?"

"It's the most important food in one of our biggest holidays," said Aviva peacefully, a small smile on her face. Inside, she could feel her heart trying to jump out of her throat, but she hoped it wasn't showing.

"This has no flavor!" the commander shouted.

"My mouth has never been so dry!"

"This is worse than the protein coagulants from the spaceship generator!"

"You really eat this?"

"We all do," Aviva said calmly. "We eat it more than once. Tomorrow is Passover."

"What about the next day?"

"That is still Passover."

The commander and his subordinate looked at each other. One didn't need the language boxes to read their body language, and Aviva knew her plan had worked.

"Get back in the kitchen. We're sending you back immediately. You're fired!" the commander barked. "Ensign, make the calculations."

"Yes, sir!"

Aviva scampered back to the kitchen and shut the door behind her, breathing heavily.

"Sorry, Chef! I'm sorry if I'm breaking your heart," called the ensign from the other side of the door. "But I have to follow his commands, you see. Try to console yourself."

"Don't worry -- I will!" Aviva called back, leaning hard against the closed door in case he tried to come inside.

There was a noise like thunder, and Aviva looked to the window. Once again she saw nighttime and palm trees. She rushed to the window and stuck her head out. The kitchen-house was restored to the palace grounds, surrounded by foliage and vegetables, just as it should be.

Pausing only to write herself a note that she needed to clean the kitchen in the morning, she hurried out of the kitchen toward Shulamit's bedchamber.

Captain Rivka was on guard duty that night. "You're up late," said the warrior in a hushed tone.

"Is she safe?" Aviva's eyes were wide, and she could barely get the words out.

Rivka's eyes twinkled. "Why shouldn't she be?" She gestured subtly at her sword. "But, go in and see for yourself."

Aviva flitted inside and approached the bed. Black, curly hair covered both the pillows; Shulamit had fallen asleep in between them. Her chest rose and fell in the peace of sleep.

Safe.

Aviva waved good night to Rivka, who shut the door, and then she took a moment to scrub herself down in case stray particles of flour had hitched a ride. When she crawled into bed, Shulamit awoke just enough to snuggle into her ample curves.

"I missed you," mumbled the little queen. She smelled of fennel seeds, which she had probably been chewing to freshen her breath just before bed.

"I missed you too," said Aviva. "I'll tell you in the morning, but I almost got stolen by the Pharaoh of Locusts."

"That's what locusts do!" Shulamit said sleepily, burrowing her face into Aviva's neck. "How did you get them to set you free?"

"I visited upon them a plague of matzo!" said Aviva with a chuckle.

END

♡ ✿ ♡

Shira Glassman is a bi Jewish violinist living in Florida with a trans guy labor activist and a badly behaved calico cat. All her books are labors of love but this one especially, since the orchestra is her other synagogue.

Shira Glassman online:
Blog: http://shiraglassman.wordpress.com
Facebook: http://www.facebook.com/ShiraGlassman
Goodreads:
https://www.goodreads.com/author/show/7234426.Shira_Glassman
Twitter: http://www.twitter.com/shiraglassman

If you liked *A Harvest of Ripe Figs*, leaving a review is probably a mitzvah.

Check out the rest of the Mangoverse!

The Second Mango
Climbing the Date Palm
A Harvest of Ripe Figs
The Olive Conspiracy
Tales from Perach/Tales from Outer Lands

Looking for excellent f/f fiction?
Check out:

Daughter of Mystery by Heather Rose Jones
Poppy Jenkins by Clare Ashton

For another book about a Jewish violinist, try Libi Astaire's *The Doppelganger's Dance*

If you're not ready to leave the tropics yet, try Zen Cho's *Spirits Abroad*

For more Jewish fantasy, try Helene Wecker's *The Golem and the Jinni*